THE PROFESSOR NEXT DOOR

CIDER BAR SISTERS, BOOK 3

JACKIE LAU

First edition: June 2021
ISBN: 978-1-989610-24-4

Editor: Latoya C. Smith, LCS Literary Services

Cover Design: Flirtation Designs

Cover photograph: Adobe Stock

[1]

"I'VE MET SOMEONE."

Nicole Louie-Edwards had been about to haul Roy into her apartment and kiss him. But then he'd placed his hand on her shoulder and uttered those words.

Not again.

Why did this keep happening to her?

The problem wasn't that she had a crush on Roy. The man was a competent lover—Nicole's standards were reasonably high —and had beefy arms that she liked to grab. They'd gotten together five times now and had fun between the sheets.

But it was just sex.

The problem? "Just sex" wasn't as easy as it used to be.

Nicole was tired of finding new partners. Tired of pulling up Tinder and hitting on men at bars. She wanted sex without the chase. Except she regularly had to find new sex partners because they kept falling in love with other women—this was the fourth time in the past year.

Why can't they fall in love with me?

Nicole shouldn't be thinking such things. It wasn't like she wanted a relationship; sex without love was better. She'd learned her lesson a decade ago. Her life now was a vast improvement over what she'd had before, but some foolish part of her wanted to be the object of someone's affections. Have the chance to gently let them down.

She forced a bright smile. "That's okay, Roy. I understand."

He ran a hand through his hair. "I knew you'd be cool about it. I wasn't looking for anyone, you know? Like I told you. But then I saw her at the wedding. Just from the back—she was wearing a gorgeous purple dress—and she was laughing. And I knew, even before she turned around."

Nicole refrained from rolling her eyes.

Love at first sight. How cute.

"Anyway," he said, "we got to talking later, and I asked her out. She said yes! We have our first date tonight. She's a teacher..."

Roy prattled on about Ms. Purple Dress, but Nicole's attention was diverted by the East Asian man walking down the hall, a duffle bag slung over his shoulder. He stopped at the unit next to hers and put his key in the lock. It was the first time she'd seen her new neighbor, though he'd lived here for a couple of months.

The man was about six feet tall and lean, with a kind but serious face. Maybe a few years older than her?

He wasn't bad-looking, but he wasn't her type. Lately, she'd been going for bulkier guys, ones who were about five years younger than her thirty-three years.

According to Mrs. Kim, he lived alone, but to Nicole, he looked like a husband. It was easy to imagine him coming home after a long day at the office and planting a chaste kiss on his spouse's cheek after slipping off his shoes. He was definitely the sort who'd work in an office, not in construction like Roy.

"Sorry," Roy said. "This probably isn't very interesting to you."

Nicole turned back to her former no-strings-attached sex partner, who was wearing a big winter jacket, unzipped, over his flannel shirt. He had cropped hair and a bushy beard.

Yeah, he was more her type.

"It's okay," she said, giving him a bland smile. "I'm happy for you. I hope you have a good date tonight."

"You're a great person, Nicole. I'm sure you'll find someone soon."

For some silly reason, her gaze strayed to the right, where her new neighbor had disappeared behind his door, before returning to Roy.

"I don't want a relationship." She just wanted a guy who'd come over to fuck once or twice a week. Was that too much to ask?

"I didn't think I did, either. And now look at me. It'll happen for you, too."

Well, Roy was high on love, how nice for him.

They said their goodbyes, and Nicole closed the door. She took off the tight jeans and slinky red shirt she'd put on for Roy and changed into yoga pants and a T-shirt. She'd wear nicer clothes when she went out with her friends tonight, but there was no need now.

Why can't I break someone's heart? Just once?

Nicole didn't actually want to hurt anyone. She just wanted to know she could be loved. Wanted to be desired for more than her looks.

But it never happened, and she was starting to feel like something was wrong with her.

No. She would not let herself feel that way. She had a job she was good at. She got along with her family and friends.

She just needed a fuck buddy who wouldn't fall in love with someone else two weeks later, and life would be perfect.

At six o'clock, Nicole pulled on her tall black boots and headed to Finch Station.

A year ago, she'd moved to this new building south of Yonge

and Finch; before that, she'd lived in the west end. It was a bit of a trek to the cider bar that she frequented with her friends, but she liked where she lived. Lots of great Asian restaurants, and it was closer to her parents and sibling.

Once on the subway, she pulled out her e-reader. At Ossington, she switched to a bus; she'd normally walk, but it was a frigid January day.

When she arrived at Ossington Cider Bar, her friends Sierra Wu and Rose Pang were already there. They had a table near the back, where they wouldn't be blasted by cold air every time someone opened the door.

"Hey, Nicole," Rose said in her cheerful, quiet voice as she pulled out a chair. "They have your blackberry nectarine cider on tap."

"Excellent," Nicole said.

"How are you?"

"Not too bad."

These were her closest friends, but Nicole didn't tell them what had been on her mind.

No, she was the kick-ass career woman who enjoyed sex and took what she wanted.

"You moved in okay?" Nicole asked.

This was the first time she'd seen her friends since Rose had moved in with Sierra, in the semi-detached house in the Annex owned by their friend Amy Sharpe. Amy had inherited it from her great aunt, but since getting married, she'd moved in next door with her husband.

Speaking of Amy...

"Hey, everyone!" Amy was perky, as usual. She pulled off her toque—complete with pom-pom—and sat down next to Nicole. "So, do I get to hear your news now, Sierra?"

"You have news?" Nicole asked Sierra. "Are you finally going to tell us who you're dating, or is it something else?"

"I'm finally telling you," Sierra said.

"You won't believe who it is!" Rose exclaimed.

"Rose already knows?" Nicole asked.

Sierra shrugged. "We live together."

"So, who is it?"

"I'm not saying anything until Charlotte arrives."

"Boo, you're no fun."

Charlotte Tam was usually punctual, but she didn't arrive for another twenty-five minutes, until Nicole had drunk half her cider and the waiter was placing a bowl of mussels in front of her. The mussels in tomato–white wine broth were delicious, and they were served with a crusty baguette and lots of butter. She slathered butter on a piece of bread and had a bite.

Then she noticed something about her friend.

"Charlotte, your shirt's inside out. And you have sex hair."

Charlotte scowled. "Goddammit. It's so hard to put on proper clothes and leave the apartment."

"Did you stop at Mike's on the way here?"

Charlotte mumbled something incoherent before heading to the washroom to fix her shirt. Nicole couldn't help but chuckle.

Once Charlotte returned and ordered one of her disgusting dry ciders, Nicole turned to Sierra. "Now will you tell us?"

Sierra wiped her mouth and had a sip of cider. "I'm dating Colton Sanders."

Nicole choked on a mussel. "*The* Colton Sanders?" she croaked.

"You mean the hotshot real estate developer?" Charlotte asked. "The billionaire?"

"Yep," Sierra said.

There was a minute of silence as they all absorbed this information, and then they bombarded Sierra with questions.

"How did you meet?"

"Does he take you on fancy dates?"

"Doesn't he have a private jet? Have you been on it?"

"Is his place on the Bridle Path really as nice as I've heard?"

"Does he treat you properly?"

The last question was Nicole's, and it sounded awfully hoarse. She still hadn't recovered from choking on that mussel.

"Don't worry," Sierra assured her. "He treats me well, and next weekend we're going to Italy together. And yes, we'll take his private jet."

Sierra had been dating this mystery guy since September. She'd probably avoided telling them because she'd anticipated all these questions.

"Isn't he, like, supposed to be the most eligible bachelor in Toronto?" Amy asked.

"Are you saying he's too good for me?"

Amy reared back. "No, no, not at all. Of course I don't think that."

Nicole didn't, either. In fact, her asshole detector went off whenever she saw pictures of Colton Sanders, but if Sierra said he was a good boyfriend, she believed her.

A part of her felt just a bit...well, sad.

Nicole wasn't envious of her friends who were coupled up, not exactly, she liked her life the way it was, but...

It's your own fault nobody falls in love with you. You have to think positive!

She shoved aside that voice in her head. Her mother's voice, even if her mother no longer had the same outlook on life that she used to.

When Nicole had been younger, she'd been made to feel like everything that happened to her was her own damn fault. There was no such thing as luck.

She didn't find herself falling into those thought patterns often now. Just occasionally.

Once Sierra had tired of answering questions about Colton and they'd all finished their meals, Nicole ordered a brownie with vanilla ice cream—because why not—plus another blackberry nectarine cider, which made Charlotte wrinkle her nose.

Charlotte, on the other hand, ordered a mocha, and after a fortifying sip of caffeine, she turned to Nicole. "Could you take me on another shopping trip? I need acceptable clothes—"

"You mean something other than pajamas and shirts with bad geology puns."

"—to wear on dates with Mike. And maybe some...you know." Charlotte lowered her voice, as though about to reveal a deep, dark secret. "Lingerie. Sexy lingerie."

Nicole's eyes widened.

"Shut up," Charlotte muttered.

"I didn't say anything," Nicole said.

"You wanted to."

"But I didn't."

"Are you going to help me or not?"

"Of course I'll help you. But the last time we went to the Eaton Centre, you said, and I quote, 'No fucking way am I going in there again, not even if I'm being attacked by a kraken. Not even if it's the only safe place in the zombie apocalypse.'"

"Pretty sure I didn't say that."

Nicole waved her hand away from her. "Close enough."

Her dessert arrived, and as she savored the warm, rich chocolate brownie, her previous sadness evaporated. She was out with her friends from university, and there was a shopping trip on the horizon. She couldn't wait to tease Charlotte about thongs and—

Why, hello, there.

A man set down at the next table. He looked like a broader version of Dev Patel, and he was checking her out, too.

Nicole winked at him.

He said something to his friends, then got to his feet.

Yes, tonight was looking up.

[2]

THUMP. *Thump.*

David Cho's neighbor was having sex.

When he'd bought this place, he hadn't realized it had such thin walls. His bedroom shared a wall with his neighbor's bedroom, and this was the fifth time he'd heard her having sex. The moaning should start right about...

"Ahhh. Yes."

...now.

He'd seen her for the first time that afternoon when he'd come back from the pool. David didn't care for the gym, but he'd been swimming laps on the weekend for years. Usually, he went earlier in the morning, but he'd been a bit late today because he'd had to do a repair job on his washing machine. When he'd returned, she'd been talking to a man just outside her door.

Until then, he'd had no idea what she looked like or how old she was. He hadn't thought too much about her appearance. Just how she'd feel in his hands, how she'd make him feel—

No! This was all wrong. Inappropriate.

He shouldn't even be listening. He should immediately head out to the living room, as he'd done the past four times. Two weeks ago, he'd read a book about the Cambrian explosion for half an hour before returning to his bedroom.

He didn't understand it. He'd heard other people having sex, and it had always made him uncomfortable, but with her, it made him both uncomfortable and turned on.

David flipped on the lights and ran a hand over his sweaty brow.

Knowing what she looked like definitely didn't help. She was a few inches shorter than him and voluptuous. She had long, dark brown hair and dark eyes, and she'd been wearing a red shirt that did great things to her ample breasts, though he'd tried not to look.

The man she was with right now—was it the white guy whom David had seen earlier? He figured there must have been at least a few men over the past several weeks, because the sounds of her partners varied, and he'd seen a different man leaving her place last month.

He thought of her as a wild, sensual, fun-loving woman. Nothing like him, in other words. Why, today, after getting back from the pool, he'd cooked lunch, done some prep for his lectures next week, and made notes on a paper he'd agreed to review. Then he'd had dinner, read a bit, and watched a movie while drinking a mug of tea.

All in all, it hadn't been a bad day, but if he'd been able to end it with her in his bed...

When he heard another moan, it went straight to his cock.

He was a thirty-nine-year-old man. He shouldn't be hard as corundum because the woman next door was having sex. It wasn't like he could even hear very much.

His imagination, however, was adept at filling in all the gaps. For some reason, his imagination was extra active where she was involved, no matter how guilty he felt about letting it run wild.

Thump. Thump.

He looked toward their shared wall and thought he detected

the tiniest movements in the rock collection on his dresser. Most things would be just fine, but the ammonite in its display stand... well, he'd have to find another spot for that.

He couldn't believe it. The sex life of his next-door neighbor was threatening the safety of his rock and fossil collection.

David moved a few choice items to his bookshelf in the living room. Better for them to be out here anyway. On the off chance he had company and that company liked rocks, it would give them something to talk about.

Having ensured the safety of his ammonite, he returned to the bedroom.

"Ohhhh."

It was her, not her partner.

David wished he could be the one who caused her to make those sounds.

A growl nearly escaped his lips, but he managed to hold it back. He didn't want her to hear him.

He padded to the washroom, leaned back against the counter, and ran his hand over his forehead again. More sweat. There was no way he'd be able to sleep if he didn't get himself off. He fisted his cock and thought of...not her.

Just another woman, maybe in her thirties, who had dark hair and lots of curves and looked very good in red. No resemblance to the woman next door, of course; that would be wrong. She was riding him, her hair curled over her naked breasts. This woman was an expert in her own pleasure. Gloried in it.

He came in his hand and stayed there for a minute, catching his breath. Then he cleaned himself up and ran a damp washcloth over his face before returning to his bedroom, which was now quiet. He checked on his rock collection before turning out the lights and falling asleep.

But at four in the morning, he was awoken from his dream about primordial soup by a thump—perhaps she should consider moving her headboard farther from the wall?—and he was immediately hard again.

God, he was too old for this.

~

Anil (last name: unknown) had been an excellent sex partner, but unfortunately for Nicole, he didn't live in Toronto. No, he lived in the US and was just in town visiting friends, so it was unlikely she'd see him again. Next time she wanted sex, she'd have to find someone new.

Too bad.

Tuesday was her birthday, and Nicole headed home alone after work. Thus far, it hadn't been a very good thirty-fourth birthday. She'd gone to a restaurant in the PATH for lunch—one she'd discovered not long after starting this job several years back, when she'd been lost. Because everyone got lost in the PATH at some point. Anyway, the food had been good today, as usual, but she'd gotten hot sauce on her blouse, which she was now hiding with a scarf.

It was terribly cold outside—the coldest day of the year, apparently. She wrapped her arms around her as she walked home from the subway station. Her teeth chattered, and snow crunched under her boots. She passed her favorite ramen restaurant, but she just wanted to go home and have a bath. Then maybe eat instant ramen.

Yes, it would be a rather sad birthday, but she reminded herself that she had plans on the weekend, and thirty-seven people had written on her Facebook wall, not that she was counting.

Five years ago, staying in on her birthday would have been unthinkable, but now...well. So it went.

Once inside her building, she checked her mail. There was a bill—she should switch this one to electronic—as well as a bright purple envelope, which made her smile. Her sibling always sent her a birthday card. Last year, to Cam's distress, it had arrived two days late.

She texted Cam. *You timed Canada Post perfectly this year!*

By the elevators, Nicole saw her new neighbor. He wore a gray wool coat and what she thought of as a dad beret, since her dad had owned something similar in her childhood. Except this beret had super cool ear flaps.

He gave her a slight smile and a nod, which she returned.

She tapped her foot as she waited for the elevator, impatient to take off these boots and drink wine in the bath. She had modest wishes for her birthday this year. No ponies or unicorns or knights in shining armor. Or a trip to Disneyland, which she'd wished for when she was six.

Her phone buzzed and she pulled it out of her purse.

Guess what? Cam said. *Po Po went viral on Twitter.*

Nicole read those words again. They didn't make sense. She hadn't been aware that her grandmother even knew what Twitter was.

A second later, Cam sent a link just as the elevator arrived. Nicole stepped onto the elevator, her neighbor following, then clicked the link. It might not load in the elevator, but dammit, she wanted to know what was going on.

Her neighbor pushed the button for the seventeenth floor, the doors closed, and they were off. Just a few more seconds until she could find out what Po Po was doing on Twitter and then get out of these clothes and—

The elevator jerked to a halt.

[3]

WHEN THE ELEVATOR stopped suddenly before the thirteenth floor, the lights went out. A moment later, another set of lights—emergency lights, David presumed—came on.

The woman standing next to him let out a hysterical laugh and muttered, "Fuck me."

The first words she'd said in his presence and they were *those* words.

She didn't mean it like that, of course, but his cheeks heated.

"Are you okay?" he asked. "Claustrophobic?"

"No, I'm fine. This just wasn't what I needed today."

David was a pro at being stuck in an elevator. Most of those times had been back in grad school. He really should have stopped taking those old elevators, but his lab had been on the top floor.

He pressed the emergency call button and recognized the voice of the man who had the evening shift at the front desk. The man said there was a power outage in the building, then mentioned something about a generator or a battery backup...

But David was having trouble paying attention because the

woman had stepped closer to him. He'd never been so close to her before, and she was scrambling his brain. How embarrassing.

He managed—sort of—to get his brain cells in working order, just in time for the concierge to tell them to sit tight for a few minutes.

The woman beside him took off her jacket, set it down on the floor, and then sat on top of it, her booted feet to one side. She wore a black skirt suit and a colorful scarf. Fancier than she'd been dressed when he'd seen her the other day. He wondered what she did for work.

David wasn't sure whether or not he should speak. What would she prefer? Was it worse to be stuck in an elevator in silence, or…? He didn't want her to feel uncomfortable.

He decided to start with sitting down beside her. She was in the process of opening a purple envelope, and when she pulled out a greeting card, she snickered. She held it up so he could see.

Hap-pea birthday to you! it said. There was a picture of three smiling green peas in a pod, each wearing a party hat.

"It's my birthday today," she said.

"Is getting stuck in an elevator interrupting any plans?" He imagined someone coming over later tonight and the noises he'd hear from next door.

"No plans, except a warm bath, wine, and instant ramen."

"Sounds better than my last birthday. It was a Friday, and I spent the evening marking midterms. And my birthday is Valentine's Day."

Even as he spoke the words, he was thinking of her in a bathtub. His brain couldn't seem to help itself where she was concerned.

No! Stop it!

It had been a while since he'd been this affected by a woman.

When she laughed, it pleased him a rather stupid amount. All he'd done was reveal the unfortunate timing of his birthday. He couldn't help wishing she'd make a subtle movement closer to him as they sat on the floor of the dim elevator. Give him a suggestive wink, a seductive tilt of her head. But he certainly didn't expect it.

"Midterms?" she said.

"I'm a professor. It was a first-year geology course."

"I had to take geology in my first year of engineering."

"Are you an engineer?"

"No. I did a degree in engineering physics, then a master's in financial math. I work on Bay Street now."

Ah. That explained the nice work clothes.

"I'm Nicole." She held out her hand, and he shook it.

"David."

"You live next door to me, I think."

"I do." *We share a very thin wall.*

~

When the elevator had halted and Nicole had sworn, David had turned somewhat pink, and she'd figured there were a few possibilities.

First of all, he could be one of those men who thought it was wrong to be alone with any woman but his wife or girlfriend, even if nothing was happening between them.

Second of all, he could be uncomfortable with swearing.

But being stuck in an elevator was definitely a situation that merited swearing, wasn't it?

The third option was that the color in his face had something to do with being stuck, like he was about to freak out. But he'd been pretty calm about the situation so far.

The fourth possibility was that she'd simply been seeing things in the crappy emergency lighting of the elevator.

Now, that seemed the most likely.

Because David—whose name she'd learned a mere five minutes ago—had been friendly, and there were certainly worse people with whom she could be stuck in an elevator. Her boss, for example, who'd have a total freak out about his time being wasted.

For a few seconds, Nicole had felt uneasy about being stuck with a man she didn't know, but David had, thus far, fit her initial impressions of him, when she'd seen him in the hallway a few days ago. The kindly husband type.

"Some birthday I'm having." She let out a rueful chuckle and looked at her phone. "I never get a signal in these elevators. I wouldn't normally care, but my grandma went viral on Twitter, and I want to see why. The link goes to a TikTok video, and dammit, I want it to load!"

He laughed, and it sounded loud in the confined space. "Your grandma's on TikTok?"

"Apparently? I feel like the whole world's been turned upside down. But come to think of it, it must have something to do with Kelsey. That's my cousin. My grandma used to live alone, but she's getting old. She refuses to go to a retirement home, though, nor will she move in with either of her daughters. So now my younger cousin is living with her. Kelsey doesn't have to pay rent, but she does have to put up with my grandma, so...who knows if it's worth it."

"Is she in Toronto?"

"Yep. My whole family is in Toronto. Well, the family I actually talk to." Some parts of her family were a mess, but she didn't need to tell the man she'd just met about that.

She adjusted her position on the floor and stared at the elevator buttons. They'd been stuck for close to ten minutes. She hadn't been worried before, but now she remembered watching a movie about three teenagers stuck in an elevator during a thunderstorm. The elevator phone was broken and nobody could hear them call for help. It had ended badly.

Next, she recalled a movie in which two people had gotten

stuck in an elevator during a storm, it had flooded, and they'd nearly drowned.

But they'd managed to escape just in the nick of time...only to be eaten by a shark. Yes, they were eaten by a shark in a parking garage.

Then there was the TV show about someone who'd fallen down an elevator shaft and lost their memory...

Don't be ridiculous, Nicole.

But wasn't it already ridiculous to be trapped in an elevator on her birthday? Not as ridiculous as being eaten by a shark in a Toronto high-rise, but still.

"You okay?" David asked.

"Just thinking of various horror movies involving elevators. Normal stuff like that."

"Well, in other movies, good stuff happens in elevators. Like, babies are born."

"Giving birth in an elevator sounds like a nightmare."

"That's fair. I'll think of something else... Sometimes people kiss in elevators, too."

It was very, very quiet.

Nicole's skin prickled, and she tried not to think of kissing David.

His cheeks turned pink again. "I'm not saying that...you know. It's just the first thing that came to mind. After giving birth. Do you want me to call the front desk again?"

She shook her head. "I'll be fine."

There was something about him that she found reassuring. Aside from those few uncomfortable seconds, he put her at ease. The sort of person who came across as stable and dependable. The sort of husband who'd come home when he said he would, who'd never fail to send a text if he was running late.

She found it hard to believe this man wasn't married.

"Do you live alone?" she asked, just in case Mrs. Kim's intel had been incorrect. "Anyone waiting upstairs who will worry about you?"

He shook his head. "It's just me."

Even though she wasn't interested in a relationship—and he seemed like a relationship sort of guy—there was some part of her that perked up at the confirmation that he wasn't living with anyone.

At that moment, the regular elevator lights came back on and the elevator jerked to life.

"Excellent," David said, standing up and picking up his coat. "Not, of course, that you were bad company but…"

She waved this off. "Don't worry, I understand."

It wasn't long before they reached their floor. Nicole stepped off the elevator and walked down the hallway with David behind her. All the lights were on, so it appeared the power outage was over.

"Happy birthday," he said as he put his key in the lock. "I hope it improves from here."

"You, too. I mean… Goodbye. It's not actually your birthday. Your birthday's in February. You told me that. But happy birthday if I don't see you again before then."

Dear God, what was wrong with her? She wasn't usually so awkward.

Well, she was having A Day.

She walked into her apartment, glad to be out of the cold weather and out of the elevator at last, and immediately looked at the link that Cam had sent her.

It was a video of her eighty-six-year-old grandmother killing a spider with a wok.

[4]

As David ate his leftover gamjatang for dinner, he kept thinking of Nicole and that birthday card with three peas in a pod. He wanted her to have a nice birthday, but he didn't want to impose.

Perhaps he could get her a cake?

After dinner, he put on his winter jacket and locked his door. At the elevators, he paused. He lived on the seventeenth floor, so taking the stairs was a little annoying, but since he didn't want to risk being stuck in an elevator again, he opened the door to the stairwell.

When he reached the street, he looked in the direction of the grocery store, but for some reason, he wanted something more special than a grocery store cake. Even though he was simply being friendly; it wasn't like he was trying to impress her and ask her on a date.

There was a Filipino bakery around the corner. He'd been in there once before, and they had lots of different things, including a selection of small cakes. That would be perfect.

When he stepped inside, the lady behind the counter scowled. "Closing in five minutes."

Right. It was nearly seven o'clock.

There was only one small cake left. It was bright purple, similar to the color of the envelope containing Nicole's birthday card.

"I'll take this one," he said.

The lady nodded, still scowling, and efficiently boxed it up and handed it over.

He returned to his building, hesitating again at the elevators before heading for the stairs. By the time he reached his floor, David was huffing. He waited for a moment, until he was breathing less heavily, before knocking on her door.

Nicole opened it right away. She'd taken off her work clothes and was now wearing flannel plaid pajama pants as well as a long-sleeved black T-shirt. It felt a little intimate to see her in such clothes, and he swallowed hard.

"I got you a birthday cake." He passed it to her. "To make up for being stuck in the elevator."

"It's not like you caused the elevator to stop. But thank you." Her face lit up as she opened the box. "Ube? From the place around the corner?"

He nodded.

"My favorite."

He was excessively pleased about that.

"You want to come in and help me with it?" she asked.

"Oh, I really shouldn't."

She took his hand and pulled him in. "I know the term just started, so you can't possibly have midterms to mark yet."

He wasn't going to decline now, and when she gestured him toward the breakfast bar, he sat down. Her unit was the mirror image of his. While he wouldn't say his place was drab, hers had bolder colors, like those red throw pillows on the couch. The décor felt a bit more modern, somehow.

She passed over her phone. "While I cut the cake, you can watch the video of my grandmother."

He started the video. It showed an elderly Asian woman hobbling toward a spider on the wall. With a wok, she gave the spider a *whack*—an impressively big whack for someone her size.

The end.

Nicole smiled. "Too bad there's no video of the time my grandma killed a garter snake in the backyard with a shovel. I was six years old, and it traumatized me. She was trying to tell me that snakes could be very dangerous, and then my dad came outside and explained that garter snakes were harmless. We saw one in the woods later, and he picked it up and tried to get me to hold it, but I refused."

She handed David a small plate with a quarter of the purple cake, then sat next to him with her own piece of cake.

She slid a forkful into her mouth. "Mmm."

Nicole probably didn't intend to be seductive when she ate, but he couldn't help being a little turned on.

He focused on his own slice of cake and had a bite.

It was, indeed, a good cake.

"Sweet enough for you?" She tossed her hair over her shoulder and winked at him.

Before he could formulate a reply, there was a knock at the door.

Who on earth could be at Nicole's door at seven thirty on a Tuesday night?

She hopped up from the stool, frankly rather pleased to get away from David. For some reason, she'd started flirting with him, even though she definitely didn't think of him in *that* way.

She opened the door cautiously, revealing Po Po and Kelsey.

"Ah, Nicole!" Po Po said. "Guess what? I got virus on the internet."

Kelsey put a hand to her forehead and shook her head. "No, Po Po. We went over this. The video went *viral*."

Po Po waved this away. "Same thing."

"Cam told me," Nicole said. "I just watched it."

"But that's not why we're here." Kelsey gave Nicole a hug. "We came for a surprise birthday visit!"

Kelsey, like Nicole and Cam, had a white father and an Asian mother—their mothers were sisters. But Kelsey's mom had lots of deeply problematic views, and Kelsey's dad was the sort of racist who claimed he couldn't be racist because of, you know, his Chinese wife and mixed-race children.

Kelsey was currently not speaking to her parents.

"Who is this?" With difficulty, Po Po took off her boots and put on the slippers that Nicole kept for her in the closet. Then she shuffled over to David.

Oh, fuck me.

Nicole had forgotten about her neighbor, who was seated at the breakfast bar and seemed unsure of what to do. If only she hadn't invited him in, or had the forethought to hide him in the closet. But how could she have known it would be Kelsey and Po Po?

Ugh, now there would be drama and family gossip.

"You are Nicole's boyfriend?" Po Po asked. Then, before he had a chance to answer, she said, "I am Nicole's po po. What is your job? How much money do you make?"

"Po Po!" Kelsey said. "You can't just walk up to men and ask about their salary. You don't even know his name."

"Ah, you are right. What is your name?"

"David."

"It is nice to meet you, David. How much money do you make?"

"He's a professor," Nicole said, "and he isn't my boyfriend. He lives next door."

"Wah, you can't be so picky. You are thirty-four now, yes?

Time to get married and have a baby." Po Po turned to David. "How many degrees do you have?"

"Three," he answered.

"See, Nicole, he has more degrees than you. You will make smart children."

How mortifying. Nicole couldn't believe she was subjecting David to this. He'd only tried to be neighborly by bringing her a birthday cake, and now he had to deal with an interrogation.

Since she didn't know what else to do, Nicole stuffed a bite of cake in her mouth while Kelsey helped Po Po sit down on the armchair.

"What kind of cake is that?" Kelsey asked.

"Ube," Nicole said. "It's really disgusting. You don't want any."

"It's disgusting? Then why are you eating it?" Po Po asked.

"She's being sarcastic," Kelsey explained.

"What is ube?"

"Purple yam. Sometimes people confuse it with taro."

Nicole looked at the remaining half of the cake. She'd planned to eat one piece for a late-night snack and another after dinner tomorrow, but she supposed it would only be polite to offer some to her family.

"Would you like to try it, Po Po?"

"Yes."

"Remember," Kelsey said, "the doctor told you not to eat too much sugar."

Po Po wrinkled her nose. "I don't care. Grandchildren refuse to get married and have babies, what is the point in living as long as I can?"

"Stop being dramatic," Kelsey said. "Besides, didn't you want to outlive Mrs. Dong?"

"You are right, I cannot let Mrs. Dong win, but I will eat just as much sugar and meat. I will live from spite! Give me the cake."

Dutifully, Nicole cut the remaining cake into thirds, deciding to save a small piece for tomorrow. She handed plates to both Kelsey and Po Po.

"Do you have any grandparents, David?" Po Po asked.

"Not living, no."

"Ah, that is too bad. Where were your grandparents from?"

"Korea. My parents came here in the seventies."

"You like BTS?"

"Po Po, you don't need to ask every Korean person if they like BTS," Kelsey said, exasperated. "Mmm. This is really good cake."

Just then, Po Po stumbled to her feet. She pulled off her slipper and slapped the wall.

"Was that another spider?" Nicole asked.

Kelsey approached the wall. "There was no spider. That was just a piece of dirt."

"You are making me look bad in front of David," Po Po said. "Why didn't you tell him that I am tough, master spider killer?"

Kelsey ignored her and turned to Nicole. "Have you watched our other TikToks?"

"Not yet," Nicole said.

"Too bad I was not wearing my cutest outfit when I killed the spider." Po Po returned to her seat. "You should have warned me!"

"How was I supposed to know there was a spider?" Kelsey asked.

"You did not plant it there for me to kill?"

"Of course not. It was a coincidence."

"Show them the other videos."

Nicole, David, and Kelsey crowded around the armchair and watched some videos. There was one of Po Po demonstrating how to make wontons, and another of her sharing tips for how to get the bill at the end of the meal.

Nicole hadn't expected David to stay, but he did.

"Do you want me to leave?" he murmured as he carried the

empty plates to the kitchen after Po Po had made sure there were no crumbs left. Wasting food was a horrible crime to her.

"No," Nicole whispered. "You're welcome to stay, but don't feel like you have to. I expect they'll be leaving soon anyway since it's almost Po Po's bedtime."

"What are you whispering?" Po Po asked. "Love words?"

"I told you," Nicole said. "We're not in love."

"Hmph. I see the way you are looking at him."

Po Po's eyes must be deceiving her.

"I will give you advice," Po Po said. "It will cost you one dollar." She held out her hand.

Nicole laughed. "Why don't you put the advice in a video instead?"

"Why won't you pay a dollar for good advice? Fine, I will give it for free. He is a nice man and he brought you birthday cake. You should date him! He looks at you the same way."

"You know, maybe you should get your eyesight checked again."

"You are wrong!" Po Po raised her finger in triumph. "I went to the eye doctor only two weeks ago. Kelsey took me. Eyes are fine."

"That's a slight simplification of what the optometrist told you," Kelsey said.

"Why you using big words?"

"Come on, Po Po. We should go. It's getting late, and I think Nicole and David were in the middle of something." Kelsey winked at Nicole, and Nicole rolled her eyes.

"I forgot about Nicole's present," Po Po said. "It's in the hallway."

Kelsey opened the door and brought in a balloon that said "Merry Christmas."

David laughed quietly, and Nicole nearly jumped. She hadn't realized he'd been standing behind her.

"Why did you get me a Christmas balloon?" Nicole asked.

"Because it was cheaper than birthday balloons," Po Po said. "Fifty percent off. If you pay me for my advice, then next time I buy you birthday balloon."

"I wish I'd been filming this," Kelsey said.

"Yes, maybe I would get a virus again."

"Go viral," Kelsey corrected.

"David, do you want me to get a virus?"

"No," he said, "I want you to stay healthy so you can bring Nicole another Christmas balloon for her next birthday."

"Will you buy another purple cake?"

"If that's what Nicole wants, then yes."

He was humoring her grandmother, and it was rather sweet, actually.

Po Po and Kelsey left a few minutes later, and Nicole pulled a bottle of white wine out of the fridge.

"I need a drink," she said as she grabbed a glass. "You want some?"

David shook his head. "I don't drink. Terrible Asian glow."

"My sibling can't metabolize alcohol properly, either. But if you don't mind, I'm going to indulge."

"Don't feel bad about drinking around me. Besides, it's your birthday."

"I can make you some tea?"

"No, I should be going, and you said something about plans for a bath."

Nicole found herself feeling a touch forlorn. She'd rather liked having him here.

She had a sip of wine. "Sorry my grandma was asking all those questions and assuming we were together."

"Don't worry about it, Nicole." He smiled at her before heading to the door.

He was going to leave, and she'd be all alone again.

"Want to come over later this week?" she asked. "We can order food and hang out, nothing big. But I don't have any friends in the building, and you're right next door."

"I'd like that."

They exchanged numbers, and then he was gone.

Nicole took her glass of wine and padded down the hallway. She set down the stemless wineglass on the edge of the bathtub and started running the bath as she stripped off her clothes.

When she stepped into the bathtub, a few tears slid down her face.

It actually hadn't been a bad birthday. She was glad she'd been stuck in the elevator. They hadn't been stuck that long, and she'd gotten to talk to David. And though she wasn't big on surprise visits, she was glad Kelsey and Po Po had stopped by. She'd rather enjoyed her grandmother's teasing, even if she wouldn't admit to it.

In truth, Nicole Louie-Edwards was lonely.

Her only real friend at the office was on maternity leave. Nicole spent most of her workday on the computer, then returned to an empty apartment.

She did like being alone sometimes, and this lifestyle had suited her for years. Besides, she had her family, and she saw her friends every week or two. She brought a guy back at least once a month.

However, in the past several months, she'd occasionally found herself wishing to come home to someone at the end of the day.

Remember Calvin.

Yes, there was a reason Nicole had switched from relationships to hookups, and that reason was Calvin Zhang. They'd lived together for two years, starting when she was in grad school. Being with him had swallowed up her identity.

But who was Nicole Louie-Edwards? Did she even really know?

There had been a few different phases in her life, and they felt like completely different people. In high school, she'd been the good student, the nerd with few friends. Now she was…what?

The sexy, lonely career woman?

She'd been happy with her life for so long, but now, things had changed.

It felt as if she was entering a new phase in her life. One in which she apparently cried in the bathtub with a glass of wine on her birthday.

Perhaps she should move and look into getting a roommate. She considered living with Rose and Sierra—there was enough room in that old house, wasn't there?

At the same time, she didn't really want to deal with roommates. She liked having her own space, and much as she loved her friends, would it be weird to live with them now? Did they only know one side of her?

Then again, what did she even know about herself?

She liked being alone at times, but she also enjoyed socializing.

She liked sex, shopping, travel, and ube cake…

Tears were still streaking her cheeks, and there was an aching loneliness in her chest, but she managed to smile as she thought of David showing up at her door with the cake. It had been so unexpected.

Did he…like her?

She immediately dismissed the possibility.

Besides, it wasn't as if she *wanted* him to like her in that way, though she still had the perverse urge to break someone's heart. For someone to say they were choosing her, rather than letting her down because they were choosing someone else.

Well, she'd see David on Friday. That would be a nice break from her regular routine.

She sipped some more wine and tried to empty her brain.

After all, it was her birthday. She shouldn't cry.

~

David slowly put away his dishes and cleaned the counters.

He thought of Nicole, having a bath. And of how meeting her grandma and cousin had compared with meeting Steph's family.

It was silly to compare. Steph had been his wife; his girlfriend at the time he'd met her family. Whereas he'd only spoken to Nicole for the first time today.

But her grandmother had thought he was Nicole's boyfriend, and she'd teased them—but she'd also seemed to approve of him.

That was a pleasant change.

It was part of the reason he'd stayed tonight, even though he'd felt a bit awkward.

If he got married again—and he hoped he would, because marriage did suit him—family was an important consideration. Never again would he agree to smile politely around bigoted in-laws. Steph hadn't shared her parents' views, but she'd only half-heartedly stood up for him.

Anyway, it had been an enjoyable evening. Nice to socialize outside of work for once. And he liked Nicole even more now, and she wanted to have dinner on Friday.

Not a date, but that was fine. He could use a friend.

The friends he'd had in Toronto had fallen into two groups: people at the university, and people who knew him through Steph. He didn't talk to the latter group anymore.

He'd never seriously considered moving back west after the divorce, though. A tenure-track position wasn't something you easily gave up, and he did like Toronto. And now he owned this one-bedroom condo, with its little den that served as his office, and spent much of the weekends alone here.

He'd enjoy a few hours a week with Nicole.

She'd given him that one slightly flirtatious look, but otherwise, there had been no sign she was interested, and he gathered she was just a rather flirty person, who looked equally lovely in both a skirt suit and pajamas.

No, she seemed to want to be friends, and so that's what he'd do.

And next time he heard noises coming from his neighbor, he'd make sure none of his rocks were in danger, and then he'd hurry out to the living room.

Or have a cold shower.

5

TO NICOLE'S DISTRESS, she was unable to have dinner with David that Friday. She had to stay at work to finish something up and didn't get home until late.

Saturday was busy, which was good. No opportunity for crying in the bathtub again.

"Here, take the last shrimp." Po Po placed it on Nicole's plate. "And tell me why your boyfriend isn't here."

"You have a boyfriend?" Mom screeched. "Why didn't I know?"

Cam looked at Nicole and chuckled. They were probably happy the relationship inquisition was off them for the moment.

Cam had recently started dating Tessa, and Nicole had hoped that Tessa would join them for Nicole's birthday lunch at her favorite Chinese restaurant in North York. Alas, Cam had claimed they didn't want to upstage Nicole's birthday by combining it with a meet-the-parents event, even though that wouldn't have bothered Nicole one bit. She very much wanted to meet Cam's new partner.

Nicole, Cam, Mom, Dad, Kelsey, and Po Po were clustered around a table in the large restaurant. It was always busy here on the weekends, full of Chinese families eating together; theirs was one of the few tables conversing almost entirely in English.

In such restaurants, Nicole often found herself searching for the white people. There were usually a few, but they were definitely in the minority. In situations where almost everyone else was white—like, say, back in undergrad—she looked for the Asian people.

Po Po was now regaling everyone with the exciting tale of how she'd met Nicole's new boyfriend, a professor who lived next door.

"We're not seeing each other," Nicole clarified. "In fact, I'd only met him for the first time an hour earlier, when we got stuck in the elevator together."

"How romantic," Cam said. "Like something out of a rom-com."

Nicole raised an eyebrow. Cam was really lovey-dovey these days. Must be because of Tessa.

"Or like a horror movie," Nicole said.

"But you made it out safely, and without any snakes eating your brain—"

"Thanks for that."

"—so clearly it wasn't like a horror movie."

"How does this thing work?" Po Po had snuck Nicole's phone out of her purse and was tapping her index finger all over the surface.

"What are you doing, Po Po?"

"I will send David a text message and invite him to lunch. Your building is not that far, so I think he can get here in ten minutes."

"David is a friend, and there's no need to invite him. He already celebrated my birthday by bringing me cake."

"He brought you *cake?*" Mom spoke as though this was the most shocking thing.

"Mm-hmm." Nicole reached for the scallops. "Po Po, can I please have my phone back?"

"No." And with that decisive word, Po Po slid the phone under her butt.

"You're sitting on my phone!"

Sitting on things was actually a special technique of Po Po's. It was her favorite way of making sure nobody could grab the bill from her, for example.

"Fine, fine." Po Po handed over the phone.

To Nicole's horror, she realized her grandmother had, after all, managed to make her phone do something.

"You butt-dialed David!" Nicole exclaimed. "Po Po!"

Since David would know she'd called, she might as well talk to him. She lifted the phone to her ear. He answered, which shouldn't please her, but it rather did.

"Hello? Nicole?" he said.

"Sorry, my grandma stole my phone and accidentally called you."

"I called him with my ass!" Po Po said gleefully.

"I wish I was filming this," Kelsey muttered.

On the other end of the phone, David chuckled. "Say hi to your grandma for me. I'll see you next Friday, okay?"

Nicole ended the call and looked around the table.

"Is he coming?" Po Po asked.

"No."

"Why not?"

"I didn't ask him."

"Give me the phone! I will butt-dial him again."

Cam was doubled over in laughter, damn them.

"It's doubtful you'll be able to repeat that," Dad said.

"This is not how smartphones work?" Po Po said. "You don't just sit on them and think about who you want to call? I thought these phones were supposed to be *smart*."

"Ma!" Mom was laughing.

"I make a joke, wasn't it funny?"

Mom, who was sitting next to Nicole, mumbled something that sounded like, "I wish she'd had a sense of humor when I was a kid."

Even though she was eighty-six and the restaurant was loud, Po Po managed to hear that. "Are you being snarky, Tammy?"

"I taught her that word," Kelsey said. "I also tried to teach her how to use Google yesterday, but that was less successful. She wanted to do research on David."

"There are lots of David Chos," Po Po said. "This is what Kelsey tells me. Most of what I saw on Google wasn't actually about him."

"Though we did find his page at the university. It has a list of publications."

"I did not understand any of the words. He must be very smart."

Nicole, too, had Googled David and found the page in question, but of course she didn't mention that this was how she'd spent her Wednesday night.

Mom put some food on Nicole's plate—even though Nicole really didn't need more food—and said, not loudly enough for the table to hear, "You don't tell me these things. Have you had a boyfriend since Calvin? Or girlfriend? Or partner? Or *special* friend?"

Nicole shook her head.

And then she looked away from her mom because she didn't want any pity.

~

"This will look nice on you." Nicole held up a pair of dark skinny jeans and a big cream-colored sweater.

Charlotte made a face. "I hate pants."

"I'm aware," Nicole said drily. "You've only told me that, like, ten bajillion times. Fine, I'll pick out a skirt for you instead."

"Nicole!"

"Then try the jeans. And the sweater's on sale, since they're making room for their spring collection."

After having lunch with her family, Nicole had met Charlotte at Fairview for shopping. They'd see the rest of their friends at the cider bar tonight.

"Oooh! Look at this!" Nicole held up a pink V-neck sweater.

"Dear God, no."

"Not for you. For me."

After Nicole picked up a gray skirt to pair with the sweater, they went to the change rooms. It was one of those places that didn't have mirrors inside the individual change rooms, so they had to come out to look at themselves.

Nicole shimmied her hips in front of the mirror. She looked good. Like a put-together woman in her thirties who got what she wanted in life. But what exactly *did* she want? She'd thought she'd known, but now, she was doubting herself.

Charlotte's outfit suited her, too. Nicole had become fairly skilled at picking out clothes for Charlotte over the years. Since she worked from home, Charlotte didn't have to dress up for work at all, but she did have to leave the apartment on occasion, to go to the grocery store and to see her friends. And, in the past few months, to go on dates with Mike Guo.

They purchased their clothes and headed to the next store.

"I think a light cowl neck sweater would look really good on you," Nicole said.

"What the fuck is that?"

Nicole held up a blue sweater. "Like this. Oooh, try this one, too." She grabbed a red sleeveless shirt with a similar neckline.

Charlotte looked doubtful, but she ended up buying both of them.

Yeah, a significant fraction of Charlotte's "leaving the apartment" wardrobe had been chosen by Nicole.

Nicole didn't buy anything at that store, but next they went to a shoe store. Now, if there was one thing Charlotte hated more than clothes shopping, it was shoe shopping, but Nicole liked shoes. She fell in love with a pair of black heels with an ankle strap, and she tried not to wince as she paid for them. They were a little expensive, and in her head, she was justifying her purchase.

But this was the great thing about being single: she didn't have to justify her decisions to anyone but herself. Her bank account was doing alright, she had savings, and she deserved a birthday present for herself, didn't she?

"Anything else you want to get before we tackle lingerie?" she asked Charlotte.

"I was thinking I could use a scarf. For decorative purposes, not for warmth."

Nicole laughed. "Okay, I know just where to go."

She ended up getting a scarf for herself, too, and then they went to the lingerie store.

Charlotte immediately laid down the rules. "I'm not trying on anything for you—I'm going to the change room by myself. I just want your suggestions. And we're only going to this one store. Nowhere else."

"Bossy," Nicole said affectionately. She held up a black teddy.

"Why are there so many holes in it?"

"To make it sexy."

"It looks like a weird lacy bathing suit. What about something more like…" Charlotte held up a white babydoll.

"Not that one. It's ugly. You prefer something with a skirt? I didn't think you would."

"It's better than *that*."

Eventually, Nicole picked out three things for Charlotte. Charlotte went into the change room and returned with two of them. She muttered something about it being wrong for small scraps of fabric to be so expensive, but she still bought them.

Nicole suggested they have coffee before heading downtown, and predictably, Charlotte's eyes lit up at the suggestion of caffeine.

They each got a coffee and sat at a table near the back of the coffee shop.

"Here, I've got something to show you. You'll appreciate this." Nicole pulled out her phone and showed her friend the video of Po Po killing a spider.

Charlotte laughed. "Oh my God, Mike would have been scared shitless. He'd have hidden in the other room while I dealt with it."

Next, they watched a series of new videos in which Kelsey showed photos of male celebrities to Po Po.

First up was Steve Yeun.

"Ah, I don't like this man," Po Po said. "He looks shifty, no? Two out of ten."

Nicole nearly choked on her coffee.

The next video showed Po Po looking at a picture of Chris Pang.

"I like him. He looks like a bit of a troublemaker, though. Maybe not the one you marry. Just the one you kiss in the bushes for fun. Eight out of ten."

This was followed by a picture of Jason Momoa.

Po Po stared at it avidly before finally uttering, "Hunky."

"I think your grandmother has similar taste in men to you," Charlotte said.

"There's so much wrong with that sentence." Nicole shook her head.

"What? She likes them big and...beefy?"

"Jesus. Stop it. She did seem to like David, though, and he's not..."

Oh, no. It appeared this coffee was some type of truth serum.

Charlotte smirked. "Did your grandma meet one of the guys you brought home?"

"David's just my neighbor. We got stuck in an elevator and he brought me a cake for my birthday. Then my grandmother stopped by unexpectedly to tell me about her TikTok success and deliver a Christmas balloon. She met him, no big deal."

Charlotte just stared at her.

"Really," Nicole said. "Nothing's happening."

Charlotte raised an eyebrow.

Nicole threw up her arms. "Oh, come on."

"Hey, after all the times you teased me about Mike, I think you deserve it. You even brought everyone to my apartment and questioned me about him!"

A valid point. However... "You and Mike are together now. And you actually wanted to date, unlike me."

"You know, I was reading some advice columns this morning."

"I thought you were laying off the advice columns because they were making you paranoid that Mike had a collection of creepy dolls and was cheating on you with a scuba instructor."

"No, no, I trust Mike," Charlotte said. "I just read them for my personal entertainment now. Anyway, there was one that made me think of you. A guy who decided to open up his marriage—well, he threatened to divorce his wife if she didn't agree to it. He arranged a swap, and the other woman was 'frigid' according to this asshole, but his wife had a great time with the other man, and now she wants a divorce."

"Yeah, I guess that's a bit like me and Calvin." Nicole sipped her coffee.

Whenever she spared her ex a thought—which wasn't often— she felt annoyed for having ever fallen for that slimeball.

When she'd met Calvin, she'd been twenty-two, and he'd been forty. At the time, she'd thought it was cool that someone so much more worldly would want to be with her.

Later, she understood: no woman close to his age would put up with his bullshit.

She knew a lot of men were nothing like Calvin, and she had a much better bullshit detector than she'd had in her early twenties.

But for the last ten years, the idea of a relationship had still made her skin crawl.

Living with someone else. Sharing finances. Having to tell them everything. Your lives so deeply entwined... Always having to consider their delicate feelings.

No, Nicole Louie-Edwards answered to no one.

"By the way," Nicole said, "you must tell absolutely no one about David tonight."

Charlotte crossed her arms over her chest and shot Nicole an assessing gaze. "Well, this is getting more interesting."

"Nothing is going on!" Nicole said, exasperated. "So I don't want to be teased."

"Maybe teasing bothers you more because you wish something was going on."

"You're not telling anyone today. It's my birthday."

"Actually, your birthday was Tuesday—"

"Yes, but today is the celebration. Don't you dare tell anyone or I'll...I'll...sing 'Happy Birthday' to you even though it's not your birthday, and you'll be so embarrassed."

"You play dirty," Charlotte said. "But, fine. Since it's your birthday celebration, and since you helped me buy all these uncomfortable—"

"But flattering."

"—clothes, I won't tell Rose, Sierra, or Amy. Just Mike."

"As long as he swears to keep his mouth shut."

Charlotte gave her another look. "You really are keyed up."

"Lunch with my family does that to me sometimes."

"I know what will make you feel better. More coffee."

"Haha, I don't want to be up all night. I don't have your tolerance for caffeine."

Charlotte kept her word. She didn't say anything to the rest of their friends about David. When Nicole teased her about her extra-dry cider, Charlotte whispered a threat but didn't follow through.

It was a fun night out with friends, and at one o'clock in the morning, Nicole got off the subway at Finch Station and walked on the snowy sidewalks back to her building.

Alone.

She hadn't seen anyone at the bar who'd interested her, and even if she had, it was doubtful she would have made a move. She'd hooked up with a guy last week; she wasn't itching for the contact just yet.

No, her vibrator—the blue one—would suffice tonight.

When she got home, she undressed and then took a minute to admire the painting in her closet. She'd had it done a few years ago. It was fucking hot, and she loved it. But she was a little too embarrassed to hang it up, even in her bedroom, because the men she brought home with her would see it. What would they think of her?

One day...

She slipped under the covers and opened the top drawer of her night table. Even though it had been a fairly good day overall, she was still feeling a little on edge.

Hopefully an orgasm would help.

6

Nicole stomped toward the elevators, both to shake the snow off her boots and also to get out her frustration that Aunt Eliza had somehow gotten her number. Ugh.

But she was looking forward to tonight.

She and David hadn't been able to make last week work, but today, he was getting dinner for them. She was supposed to be at his place, well…five minutes ago.

When David answered the door, she smiled. Just seeing his face calmed her, even if he reminded her of being stuck in an elevator. It was nice to have a friend in her building.

"I got bibimbap," he said. "I hope that's okay."

She nodded. "Sounds good."

He gestured to a chair at his breakfast bar. In front of it, there was a round takeout container, a small handle-less teacup, and metal chopsticks. He poured her tea as she took a seat.

It was nice to come home and have someone take care of her.

Not that this was home, but it was right next door. And not that he'd done all that much, really. It wasn't as though he'd spent hours in the kitchen. But still.

She took a sip of her steaming tea, then pulled the lid off her container and started furiously mixing everything up with her chopsticks.

She felt David's gaze on her.

"What?" Perhaps she sounded huffy, but she didn't mean to.

"Rough day at the office?" he asked.

"No, work was okay. The usual. But I was just about to leave when my aunt called, and my aunt and I aren't on speaking terms."

"Oh?"

"She's racist and transphobic. And…" Nicole shook her head as she reached for some kimchee. "Mom, Dad, my sibling, and I don't speak to her. Kelsey, who's her daughter, doesn't talk to her, either. Po Po is always trying to mend fences between Mom and Aunt Eliza, but that's not happening."

David sipped his tea in silence, as though waiting for her to continue.

"Anyway, you know how my grandma's on TikTok? Well, she appeared in a listicle. 'Best TikTok grandparents' or something like that. Aunt Eliza saw it and is furious that Kelsey would put videos of Po Po online, but Po Po knows what's going on and consents to it. She thinks it's great fun, and people love her."

Before the unfortunate call from Aunt Eliza, Nicole had gotten a call from Po Po, who was so pleased to be on a "Popsicle."

"So, Aunt Eliza wants me to convince Kelsey to take all the videos down, especially the one where Po Po is practically salivating over Jason Momoa."

Beside her, David put a bite of food in his mouth and laughed quietly.

There was something about his laughter… It was a nice laugh, and it made her smile.

He was wearing navy pants, a maroon sweater, and a collared shirt. Probably what he'd worn to work.

Where was she again…? Right.

"I told Aunt Eliza that she better not call this number again, and that there's nothing wrong with those videos. Then I managed to stop myself from slamming the phone down and cracking the screen."

"You showed great restraint," he murmured.

"Do you think it's terrible that I refuse to talk to my aunt?"

"No, it's good to set boundaries with awful people. I trust your judgment."

"But you hardly know me."

He shrugged. "Am I wrong?"

"You're trusting me to judge my own character? No, you're not wrong." She picked up a piece of beef. "How was your day?"

"Well, I didn't have to speak to anyone in my family, just lots of students. Friday is a busy teaching day."

"Do you like teaching?"

"It's not something that comes naturally to me," he said. "I mean, standing at the front of a room, projecting my voice, everyone's eyes on me."

"Aside from the ones who are sleeping."

"Before a lecture, I feel like I'm getting into character. I've gotten better at it over time, though, and I rather enjoy teaching now."

She had a feeling that he would try very hard to do a good job of it.

They finished their meals, and David poured more tea and brought out a small box from a bakery. He opened it to reveal four egg tarts, but not the sort she was used to getting at dim sum or Chinese bakeries. These had brown spots on the top.

"They're from a Portuguese bakery downtown," he explained. "Would you like one, or should I keep them all for myself?"

She gave him a gentle shove. "Stop teasing me."

She picked up a tart and put it as far from him as she could reach. He laughed. Then she placed the other three tarts beside the first tart.

"Nicole."

His slightly stern tone made her squeeze her thighs together.

She tried not to think about that as she put two tarts back in the box and allowed him to try the dessert he'd so kindly bought for them.

The tarts were delicious. She closed her eyes to savor the silky filling, and when she opened her eyes again, David was giving her a peculiar look.

A look that men had certainly given her in the past, but David...nah.

Must be her imagination.

"You know," she said, "I think I like these more than the Hong Kong–style ones."

After two egg tarts, Nicole was quite full, and at the same time, she felt more at ease than she had in a while. This dinner had relaxed her, rather like an orgasm.

She put a hand to her mouth as though she'd said it out loud, but she hadn't.

David raised his eyebrows, and even though she was rarely embarrassed, she could feel her cheeks heating.

For some reason, she thought back to the days after she and Calvin had broken up. She'd been living by herself for the first time, and she'd loved it. Nobody telling her what to do or expecting her to be free at awkward times. She could spend as much time as she wanted on whatever she wanted, and no one was there to judge her. She could eat in front of the TV, stay up late watching movies, do the dishes when she felt like it. Nobody would know if she ate most of a pint of ice cream. No one would ask where it all went.

After so many years of living with other people—her family, other university students, then Calvin—it had been a novelty. She wished she could recapture that feeling.

But now, eating dinner with someone else in her building seemed like a novelty.

She felt slightly unsettled, but still more relaxed than she had earlier. Her aunt's phone call was a distant memory.

She chatted with David for a little longer. They made plans to meet again next week, and Nicole found herself looking forward to a simple dinner far more than she ought to.

On Wednesday, David was checking his mail—nothing but a flyer he didn't want—when someone said his name from right behind him. He startled and dropped the flyer.

"Sorry," Nicole said, reaching to pick it up.

They headed to the elevators together, and he tried not to stare at her. She wore a long winter jacket and a black beret tilted on her head. It looked stylish and sophisticated on her, whereas his hat had ear flaps.

It baffled him that she was giving him her Friday evenings.

Although maybe she went out afterward. Their dinner together could be just the start of a long night, and then she'd meet friends for drinks.

He hadn't heard any noises through the wall last weekend, though that didn't mean she hadn't brought someone home. It was possible to have sex in places other than the bedroom...

No, he shouldn't be thinking about that.

The elevator doors opened and they stepped on. This was the first time they'd taken the elevator together since they'd gotten stuck.

She made a show of holding her breath as they approached the thirteenth floor, then released it when they got to their floor.

"Success." She smiled at him over her shoulder.

God, she was gorgeous. No one should be able to make a beret and winter coat look that good.

"David?" she said, putting her hand on the elevator doors to hold them open. She'd stepped onto their floor, but he was still on the elevator, flustered.

He didn't usually think of himself as the absent-minded professor.

"Right." He walked out of the elevator and followed her down the hall.

There was something about Nicole that always made her seem sophisticated, even the time he'd seen her in pajamas. Put together, but not like she was showing a mask to the world. No, not at all.

He liked that, the contrast between the sounds he could hear from her bedroom on occasion...and the woman walking in front of him now.

"See you on Friday." She gave him a little wave as she put the key in her lock.

"See you," he said.

~

On Thursday at five o'clock, David was in his office, considering a little light cleaning. His office wasn't in bad shape; it wasn't one of those offices with papers and books everywhere, teetering towers that threatened to collapse at any moment.

Not that he made fun of Murray for that.

Well, not too much.

Professor Murray McRae, who was nearly two decades older than David, was his closest friend in the Department of Earth Sciences. Murray had been very welcoming when David had started at the university, in part because he was pleased that David was taking over teaching his first-year class.

Anyway, David usually left around five or five thirty, but the two times he'd run into Nicole had been when he'd left later than usual. Yesterday, it had been thanks to a curriculum meeting.

Maybe he'd start coming in later than eight in the morning and leaving—

No. He was acting like a schoolboy with a crush, even though it was less than two weeks until his fortieth birthday.

He didn't need to resort to changing his schedule just so he had a chance of running into Nicole and spending two minutes with her. She was having dinner with him tomorrow.

But those shelves sure did look dusty...

He put his glasses on and took a closer look.

No, he couldn't justify it to himself.

He left work right away and didn't see Nicole by the elevators, which was more of a disappointment than it should have been.

7

FRIDAY AFTER WORK, David knocked on Nicole's door, his heart beating a touch fast.

She opened the door and smiled at him. She was wearing lounge pants and an off-the-shoulder blue shirt, and she managed to look like she could be in an ad.

"I brought dessert." He held out a small box.

She'd said she would figure out dinner this time, but they hadn't discussed dessert. He hoped this didn't ruin her plans.

But she looked delighted when she opened the box.

He'd spent an embarrassing amount of time researching places to buy dessert in the area. The pastries weren't large, but they'd likely be very rich. One was full of chocolate in many different forms, and the other—

"What's this?" she asked, pointing at the white and orange one.

"Mango mousse, white chocolate, and coconut."

"Ohh."

She really did him in when she made noises like that.

Nicole took lots of pleasure in her food. Like she took pleasure in...

Stop it.

She'd given no indication that she saw him that way, and he wouldn't make things weird. He suspected if Nicole wanted someone, she'd be very clear about it, and he liked that about her.

No, he realized now that she was a little lonely, like he was.

And he hated that she'd be lonely.

"What did you get for dinner?" he asked.

"Dan dan noodles from the Sichuan place a few blocks south."

She served the noodles into bowls and passed him chopsticks as well as tea. After pouring herself a glass of red wine, she sat down beside him and groaned as she had her first bite of noodles.

"Good?" he asked mildly.

"*So* good. I haven't had these in months—I don't know why. I used to go every two weeks when I first moved here."

"How long have you lived in this building?"

"A year."

He nodded. "I used to live closer to the university, but when I decided to buy…"

"Oh, you own your place? I don't."

"I bought it after I got tenure."

"I should look into buying something. Real estate is so expensive in Toronto, but I think I could afford it now. There's something that's stopping me from doing it, though, and I'm not quite sure what."

He didn't want her to move. He wanted her to stay right next door.

But, of course, he didn't say that.

There was a pause in conversation as she enjoyed her noodles and sipped her wine. It was terribly erotic to watch her eat. To watch her enjoy herself.

Stop lusting after her!

"How was your week?" he asked. "Any news from your family? Did your grandma show up with more Christmas balloons?"

She chuckled. "No, but she and Kelsey recorded a short dance."

"To which song?"

"I don't know! Something very popular with young people. I guess I'm too old to know these things now. What about you? How was your week?"

He didn't know what to tell her. His life sounded so *boring*. But it didn't seem like she expected anything exciting.

"Um," he said, "I found a good poke place near campus?"

When it came time for dessert, Nicole decided she wanted to try both pastries, so she cut them each in half. She alternated between bites of the two desserts.

"Did you like them?" he asked once she'd finished eating. He couldn't help feeling nervous, as though her verdict was of the utmost importance.

"Mmm, yes. They were really good." She licked some of the mango mousse off her lips, and it seemed slow and sensual to him, but she probably wasn't thinking about that at all.

"Which did you prefer?"

She tilted her head to one side. "I couldn't possibly decide. Guess I need to eat more to help me figure it out."

Playfully, she reached for his plate; he still had a few bites left.

He pulled the plate back.

She reached for it again, and he was almost about to let her have it, because even if he had a weakness for sweets, he had a bigger weakness for her. That silly schoolboy crush.

He let go of the plate, then realized she didn't have a steady grip on it.

The small plate tumbled to the floor, where it shattered.

"Oh my God," she said. "Oh my God. I'm so sorry."

"It's yourself you should be sorry to. I was going to let you eat it. And it's your dish, and it fell on your floor."

Nicole looked at the plate on the floor, then looked back at him.

She had a gulp of wine and started laughing, covering her mouth so the wine didn't spew out. She finally seemed to swallow, but then she snorted, which made her laugh more.

There was something about her being so unselfconscious that made him smile, and then he was laughing along with her.

"This is what I get for being greedy." She hopped off the chair and started cleaning up the mess. "Don't worry, I'll make sure you get your pastries."

She winked at him over her shoulder, which he found flirtier than he should.

The next day, when David returned from the pool, he found a small box in front of his door. There were two pastries inside. The same ones he'd bought for Nicole the previous night, except they were half the size of the ones the bakery served. Bigger than what he'd had left before the little accident last night, though.

There was a small handwritten note inside the box.

Here's your share, she'd written, followed by a little heart.

Did that heart mean something?

Surely not.

Still, he didn't throw out the note.

≈

As Nicole indulged in late-morning pastries, she started to have regrets.

She'd ended that note with a heart, hadn't she?

She groaned.

After finishing her pastry and coffee, she tiptoed out of her unit and into the hallway, as though going on a secret expedition.

She looked over at his door. The box was already gone.

Dammit.

≈

At their next Friday dinner, Nicole thought David might say something about the note, but he didn't—he just thanked her for the "suspiciously small" pastries—and she was glad. Her brain had made a little slip-up, that was all. Perhaps he hadn't even noticed the heart.

Besides, it was hard to obsess about it too much when she was eating this incredible moussaka. The bechamel sauce was rich, so she wouldn't be able to eat a ton of it, but...

Oh, who was she kidding. She was eating this whole piece.

She'd just set down her fork when the phone rang. Her grandmother.

"Go ahead and answer it," David said. "I don't mind."

She picked up the phone. "Hi, Po Po."

"Did you see me, Nicole? I was in another Popsicle."

"Listicle, Po Po."

"Ah, whatever, they are all the same. Eliza says videos are *inappropriate*, but she is being silly. They are so much fun. Kelsey reads me comments. People say I am cute! What are you doing right now?"

"Just finished dinner."

"Can I speak to David? I want to ask him a question."

What could Po Po possibly want to ask—

Wait a second. How did Po Po know she was with David right now?

"David's not here."

He gave her a look, and Nicole smothered a laugh.

Though apparently, she didn't do a good enough job of it.

"He is definitely there," Po Po said. "That's why you are laughing."

"No, he's not."

"Fine, fine, keep lying to your po po. Just make sure he does something nice for you on Valentine's Day, yes? It's on Sunday."

"Yes, I know."

"He should get you a big bouquet of the prettiest flowers."

"I'll tell him."

"Okay, I will let you go now because I think you are on a date."

"It's not a date..." Nicole trailed off. Her grandmother had hung up the phone.

She turned, then realized David was no longer beside her. He'd stood up to get something out of the fridge.

"Cheese tart for dessert," he said. "They opened a new location of Cheese & Me at Empress Walk last month. Do you wanted it chilled, or should I heat it up?"

"I like cheese tarts warm."

She tried not to drool, but when the large tart came out of the oven, she couldn't help it. She wiped her mouth with a napkin, hoping David didn't notice.

And when she broke off a piece of the crust and dipped it in the middle of the tart...

OMG.

"This is amazing," she said, being rude and speaking with her mouth full.

"I'm glad you like it." He sounded very serious about that, like it was very important to him that she enjoy this tart.

There was only one tart, so they shared—it certainly ought to be big enough for two. If Nicole hadn't eaten all that moussaka and pita with baba ganouj, she could have eaten the whole thing, but as it was, she was full, and she didn't want to deprive David of his share of dessert, like she'd done last week.

These dinners had been an excellent addition to her life. David was a relaxing person to spend time with, unlike her family, much as she loved them. And he kept supplying her with excellent desserts.

She'd been feeling less lonely these days, though there were still moments...

All she needed in her life now was a no-strings-attached sex partner.

She put that thought aside as she remembered something. "Sunday is Valentine's Day, which means it's also your birthday."

"It is indeed."

"Do you have plans?"

He shook his head.

"We should do something!" The words were out of her mouth before she'd thought it through. "When was the last time you went out, other than having a poke bowl for lunch? That doesn't count."

"I think I had dinner with another prof early in January?"

"David," she scolded. "You need to get out! You go out even less than my friend Charlotte, which is quite a feat. Though Charlotte does work from home, and you must see lots of people at work."

"Going out on my birthday has always been a little awkward since it's Valentine's. Restaurants are busy."

"We won't go out for dinner. We'll do lunch. You can pick the restaurant, how about that?"

Nicole left an hour later and began the arduous trek—ha!—back to her apartment.

For the first time in years, she was really looking forward to Valentine's Day.

[8]

It was strange being in a restaurant with David.

Thus far, their relationship—their platonic relationship—had consisted of going over to each other's apartments to eat, but now here they were, out in public.

Nicole felt slightly disoriented.

Maybe that was more because she was actually out at a restaurant with a man on Valentine's Day than anything else.

It was a Japanese restaurant that specialized in udon. David's choice. She had a sip of water, picked up her menu, and—

"Oh my God," she whispered.

David glanced up at her. "Did you say something?"

She looked down at her menu so she didn't stare at him.

"You wear...glasses," she stammered.

"For reading, yes." He sounded amused at her reaction, but she didn't dare look at what was written on his face.

Because for some reason, she found him really fucking attractive with glasses. They were dark frames, nothing fancy, but...

What was happening to her?

She squirmed in her seat and gripped the menu. She really

needed to get laid. That must be why David in glasses was making her flushed.

In Nicole's experience, if she wasn't particularly attracted to someone when she met them, it was unlikely to change. So the fact that her mouth was dry and her skin was hot... Yeah, that must just be because she hadn't had sex for a while. Nothing to do with David.

Satisfied with her reasoning, she skimmed the menu, but she couldn't stop herself from sneaking covert glances at him. He was studiously reading his menu and probably retaining more information than she was.

"What are you thinking?" he asked.

"The, um, udon." She still had no idea what the menu said; she just knew there were many udon options.

"I'm getting the curry udon with tonkatsu."

"I, uh..."

She was distracted when he brushed an errant piece of hair out of his eye. He needed a haircut, and she suspected he would get one soon, as David didn't seem like the sort who'd put off something he needed to do.

Finally, she managed to concentrate on the menu for a full minute.

"I'm going to have the cheesy baked udon," she said at last. It came with shrimp, and it sounded decadent.

He nodded, as though approving of her choice, and she squirmed in her seat again.

After the waitress took their orders, David put his glasses away, and Nicole finally felt like she could breathe again.

Yep, for next weekend, her priority would be having sex.

She clinked her water glass against David's. "Happy birthday. What number?"

"Forty," he said.

"Oh, wow. That's a big birthday. And to think, if it wasn't for me, you wouldn't have gone out at all. Good thing you've got me as your neighbor."

"Yes. Fortunate indeed."

Thump. Thump.

David had been about to doze off when the thumping startled him into alertness.

There were some muffled words, which might have been "Just like that," but they could also have been something completely different.

He hurried out to the living room, but the knowledge that Nicole was right next door, having sex…likely naked…

Or if she wasn't naked, her dress might be hiked up, her panties pushed to the side.

Fuck. He was already semi-hard.

He headed to the washroom, in desperate need of a cold shower. When he shucked off his clothes and stepped under the cold spray, he couldn't hear her anymore, but he still kept picturing her.

He would think of something else.

Food. Yes, food.

Those long, cheesy noodles disappearing into her mouth last Sunday. Her lips wrapped around the straw in her drink, and then around the single cherry…

Yesterday, she'd gotten pizza for their Friday dinner. Pizza with extra cheese. Nicole loved cheesy and creamy foods, and whenever she ate cheese, she moaned in appreciation.

It drove him mad.

He thrust his fingers through his wet hair. It had been a while, but he remembered cold showers being more effective than this. Tonight, however, he still felt unhinged.

But when he was with Nicole, he tried his best to be calm and composed. He didn't let on how sensual he found it when she ate. Didn't let on how badly he wanted to kiss her.

What if she's thinking the same thing?

No, he doubted it very much.

David might be the sort to silently crush on someone for months and months—this hadn't changed much from his school days—but Nicole wasn't.

He was quiet and introverted, though he didn't generally consider himself a shy person. However, when he didn't think his feelings were reciprocated, or had no idea, he was shy.

Despite being in the shower, he was still able to faintly hear a moan.

Fuck.

He couldn't see her. He could only hear her...barely. Why did it turn him on so much?

He wanted to see her with her lips around his cock, enjoying having him in her mouth as much as she enjoyed those egg tarts.

No, no, don't think of her giving you a blowjob! She's your friend.

Usually, the fact that something was *wrong* didn't turn David on.

But now...

He made the shower even colder. As cold as it would go. He wasn't as hard, and he was practically shivering, but he still couldn't help his lustful thoughts.

She thought he was a kindly academic, and instead, he was getting aroused when she put food in her mouth. Fantasizing about sinking inside her body and grabbing her plump ass.

He felt like a fucking horny teenager. He couldn't take this anymore.

Annoyed, he turned off the shower, dried himself off, and by some miracle—really, it was a miracle—managed to fall asleep.

When he awoke the next morning, he decided he'd have to tell Nicole the truth.

Part of it, anyway.

~

David had thought something without melted cheese would be less sensual, so he'd gotten red curry from a Thai restaurant.

Unfortunately, Nicole kept making expressions of delight that he still found erotic.

He figured he'd wait until they were done dinner to say what he needed to say. He'd just let her know that the walls were probably thinner than she thought, and he could hear her; she could adjust her behavior as she desired. That was it. He didn't want to shame her.

And then he'd figure out how to stop his dirty thoughts about her, once and for all. He felt incredibly guilty about his lack of control over his imagination.

"David?" she said.

Oh, had she asked him a question? Shit.

"Sorry," he said. "It's been a long week. It was Reading Week before that, but now it's back to teaching and the midterm was on Wednesday."

He wasn't sure she believed his excuse, but she let it slide. They hadn't known each other long, and they didn't push answers out of each other.

When they finished their meal, he cleared the dishes and brought out dessert.

"Happy As Pie," Nicole said, reading the logo emblazoned on the box. She opened it up. "You got us a whole pie?"

"Pear ginger crumble pie," he said, his voice scratchy. "You can take the extras home."

"Oh, no. I couldn't take them all. We'll split it."

"I bought ice cream, too." He grabbed the vanilla ice cream from the freezer and took a deep breath. Okay, this was it. "I have to tell you something."

"Yes?"

"I can hear you. Having sex, I mean."

[9]

"YOU CAN HEAR ME HAVING SEX." Nicole had been about to cut them each a slice of pear ginger crumble pie, but now she dropped the knife.

"Yes." David set down the pint of ice cream and raked a hand through his hair. "The walls are thin in this building, and I hear when you shower, and when the guy on the other side of me blasts The Hip, but I can also hear when you have sex. As your friend, I thought you should know. So that if you don't want anyone to hear, you can be quieter or move your activities to another room, that's all. Maybe shift your headboard farther from the wall, not that this would stop certain...noises."

David was stumbling over his words and turning red.

She found it incredibly cute.

Then she looked down at his forearms. He'd rolled up the sleeves of his blue button-down shirt. His arms weren't huge, but they were somehow especially pleasing.

"Does the noise bother you?" she asked.

"I, well...it's not like it's super loud. If you don't want to change anything, it's fine, just know that I can hear."

"Do you listen?"

"What? No. I leave the room. It would be wrong for me to listen." He spoke forcefully, and his Adam's apple bobbed as he swallowed.

She couldn't help feeling disappointed.

The other day, she'd found herself strangely turned on when he'd put on his glasses, and now, she was feeling turned on again.

She didn't understand it. He wasn't her type, not at all. She normally went for more muscled guys with broader shoulders. Guys who weren't at all uncomfortable talking about sex.

David seemed to be struggling, though. Conversation was usually easy between them, but now he was setting out small plates for dessert and trying not to look at her.

And somehow, she found this adorable?

She gulped her tea and was suddenly very aware of his long fingers, placing the ice cream scoop into the pint. She felt unsteady in a way she hadn't in a long time, but then a thought snuck into her head.

The reason David looked so nervous was because he *wanted* to listen...right?

Ooh, she could have fun with this.

Feeling more confident, she cut them each a generous slice of pie, and he scooped out the ice cream. They worked as a team in silence.

She slid the first bite of pie and ice cream into her mouth.

"Mmmm." She drew out her sound of pleasure. Just a slight exaggeration—it really was good pie.

David's eyes were laser-focused on her lips...and then he looked away.

"Thank you for telling me," she said at last.

"You're welcome," he mumbled.

"I think you want to listen."

His gaze snapped up to hers.

They usually sat beside each other, but after getting the plates, he'd stayed on the other side of the counter, standing, as he ate his pie.

"I..." He shook his head.

She was reveling in her power.

But then something occurred to her. "Wait a second. Is that why you wanted to get to know me? Because you could hear me having sex, and you could see men leaving my apartment, and you thought I was easy? Is that why you brought me that ube cake?"

He looked horror-struck by her words.

"No, no," he said. "I liked talking to you, and it's nice to spend time with someone in the evenings. This isn't all a plan to... *No.*"

Nicole started to relax. She believed him, and she didn't think she was naïve to do so. She'd spent quite a bit of time with David over the past few weeks, and she couldn't see him lying about something like this. Plus, he seemed so gosh darn uncomfortable with the conversation.

A burst of laughter escaped her lips as she tried to imagine David *talking dirty.*

He raised his eyebrows but said nothing.

Very much a *David* response.

She wasn't accustomed to sleeping with people whom she considered friends; she tended to keep friendship and sex separate. But sex with David would be very convenient, if it could be a regular thing. Convenience wasn't something she used to care about as much, but in her mid-thirties, it sounded awful nice. He was right next door.

Nicole looked down at her dessert. Usually, she inhaled the desserts that David bought, but today, she'd been lost in thought. Her vanilla ice cream was melting.

She put a bite of pie in her mouth and tilted her head. When she slid the spoon out of her mouth, she did it very, very slowly.

She was good at this shit. She knew she was.

And David wasn't immune. His inhale was quiet, but she

could hear it nonetheless. She'd become attuned to little changes in him, and affecting this kind, calm man...it was thrilling.

"You do want to listen, don't you?" she said.

"Um."

"Are you always a bit of a voyeur?"

He shook his head decisively.

Interesting.

"Well, if you hear me having sex again," she said, "I give you permission to listen and jerk yourself off. Picture me naked. Whatever you like."

The thought of David lying in bed, wearing those cute glasses because he'd been reading...

Why were the glasses doing it for her? They'd never been a turn-on for her before.

Anyway, she pictured him reading in bed at midnight, then hearing her next door, setting his book aside, and reaching down to stroke his cock.

Oh, God.

It had only been a week, but she *so* needed to get laid.

"What about the other person?" he asked.

"I'll let him know that my neighbor will likely hear and enjoys listening, don't worry. If he doesn't like that idea, there's always the couch."

For the past several months, although Nicole had still enjoyed sex, she'd been tired of the chase. Tired of flirting.

But now, she was excited again.

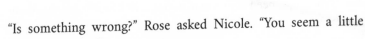

"Is something wrong?" Rose asked Nicole. "You seem a little distracted today."

Nicole sipped her passionfruit peach cider. She loved this one. Passionfruit tasted good in everything, and the sweetness—though it had a nice bite, too—offended Charlotte.

"No, I'm fine," Nicole said.

There was nothing *wrong*, that was true, but yes, she was a bit distracted. She kept scanning the cider bar, looking for the right man to seduce.

Fuck, she was horny.

It had taken her a while to get ready tonight, and she'd eventually settled on a ruched, deep blue dress and silver jewelry. She was more dressed up than everyone else at the table—particularly Charlotte, who was wearing jeans and a big sweater.

Charlotte's boyfriend, Mike, was here tonight, as was Amy's husband, Victor, and Mike looked at Charlotte like she hung the moon in the sky or some such nonsense.

Though for a moment, Nicole wished someone would look at her that way, too…

No, what she really craved was for someone to fuck her up against the wall.

A group of men sat down at a nearby table, and she gave them a perusal. One was similar to the sort of man she usually went for, but nah, he wasn't quite right.

She returned her attention to her friends.

"So, you all want to meet Colton?" Sierra asked.

"Yes!" Amy screeched, then put a hand over her mouth. "I've been begging you for weeks."

"Well, he wants to meet you all, too. I'll figure something out soon."

Although Nicole was curious to meet Colton, she couldn't help worrying about this privileged, rich white dude. Then she reminded herself that Sierra had better taste in partners than she did. Calvin had been a supreme douche, but Sierra's ex-husband had been a decent guy. Not the right man for Sierra—he was happily married to someone else now—but not a bad person. Plus, Sierra had assured them all that Colton was good to her.

Even if that was true, Nicole still feared that Colton would change Sierra, that she would lose a bit of herself to the relationship.

Though that hadn't happened to Charlotte. She was still an antisocial grump, which was nice to see.

"Here you go, dear sister." A waitress placed a glass of cider in front of Charlotte.

Their waitress tonight was Julie, Charlotte's younger sister. She couldn't stay and talk, though, as the bar was quite busy—it was usually busy on Saturdays.

Yet there were no men who interested Nicole.

"You know what you should do," Amy said to Sierra. "Since Colton's so rich and well-connected, you should ask him to get tickets to the world premiere of your movie."

They called it Sierra's movie because Sierra shared her name —first and last—with the main character. The movie was based on the first book in a very popular urban fantasy series, which just so happened to be Amy's favorite series ever.

"Make sure he gets a ticket for me," Amy added.

As they talked about the casting in the movie, Nicole's eyes drifted around the bar again.

That was when she saw him.

A big white guy, maybe a few years younger than her, sitting at the bar with a couple of friends. He had sandy brown hair, a big beard…and glasses.

She didn't dwell on why the latter was really working for her. Instead, she adjusted her dress and stood up.

"Excuse me," she said to her friends with a wink.

She strutted toward him, and when he looked up, she ran her tongue over her upper lip.

His gaze was riveted on her.

Oh, yes, Nicole Louie-Edwards was *back*.

And she had the mild-mannered professor next door to thank for this.

~

Thump. Thump.

David had been lying in bed and reading for the past hour, waiting for that noise while simultaneously telling himself he was *not* waiting for it, even though he'd been thinking about it for the entire day. Nicole didn't have sex every Saturday, after all...

Thump. Thump.

"*Ohh.*"

It was slightly louder than usual. Was she doing that for him?

He shouldn't flatter himself.

But she'd turned up the sex appeal last night. She'd been purposefully eating her dessert in a seductive manner—and he already found it hot when she wasn't trying to be seductive.

That wasn't how he'd expected her to respond when he revealed what he could hear. Maybe a little giggle and an, *Oh, I didn't realize the walls were that thin. I'll keep it in mind.* Unlike him, she wouldn't stammer, and maybe she'd be a bit embarrassed, but not too much.

Instead...

After setting down his book and glasses, he slipped his hand inside his boxers. It felt like he was doing something illicit, and David wasn't used to feeling this way. He was a play-by-the-rules guy.

But she'd told him he could listen, so this wasn't wrong, and for once, he wouldn't try to rein in his thoughts.

He fisted his cock, imagining it was her hand on his cock instead, and she was naked, her hair tumbling over her shoulders. She'd beg him to touch her, not at all shy about what she wanted, and he'd comply. He'd find her wet, so wet for him. She'd offer him her breasts, and he'd suck on her nipple while his fingers were buried in her pussy.

God, yes.

Then he'd fuck her hard with a toy—he bet she had a nice

collection to satisfy her needs—while he licked her clit, and she'd take it. She'd love it when he gave it to her good. She'd make those sounds, those moans…

Like the ones he was hearing right now

They were followed by more thumping.

David imagined he was on top of her, fucking her. Her hair fanned out on the pillow, her lips parted, her breathing hard.

The expression of absolute pleasure on her face.

He wanted to know *exactly* what she looked like when she was in the throes of passion. Fuck, he'd give anything to see it.

This woman who loved sex…he bet she'd be fucking gorgeous.

"Ohhhh. Yes."

That was her. Climaxing?

He stroked himself more furiously.

Thump. Thump. Thump. Thump.

And then…silence.

He was still stroking himself, because he'd been holding off, not wanting to finish too soon, but now—

Then there was a knock on the wall.

A fucking *knock*, different from those thumps.

He spent himself in his hand.

10

THE NEXT DAY WAS A SUNDAY, which meant David went to the pool.

He'd never been much for sleeping in, at least not in the past decade. Back when he was a teenager—a horribly long time ago now—he might have been able to sleep until ten.

But now, sleeping in was seven thirty.

It was a twelve-minute walk to the pool, and he was there by eight. As he came out of the change room, he nodded at the older gentleman whom he regularly saw swimming laps, then climbed into the pool.

Swimming usually helped clear his mind, and today, he desperately needed that. Ever since Friday evening, his thoughts had been filled with Nicole.

As he started swimming, his brain was still consumed with her, but a half hour of exercise should be enough to get her out of his mind, right?

She knocked on the wall.

He still couldn't get over that, and he wondered how much she'd been thinking of him yesterday, when she was with another man.

It wasn't the idea of her being with someone else that turned him on; he just wanted to see her enjoying herself.

Preferably with him.

David had always considered himself a poor flirt. He worried not only about making a fool of himself, but also about making the other person uncomfortable, and so flirting was just something he didn't do.

But he could do a very good job of making out and having sex —at least, he liked to think so—because he was good at paying attention and listening.

He just didn't get to that point often. For example, in the four years since his divorce, he'd been with one woman.

What did Nicole want? Did she want to sleep with him? Or was she just turned on at the idea of someone listening? Was she a bit of an exhibitionist?

And what did *he* want?

Well, it was pretty simple. He just wanted *her*.

It was hard to think beyond that, beyond having her wet and willing beneath him.

When he got home at nine, he was still thinking of her. His swim hadn't calmed his thoughts. And when he stepped into the shower to wash off the chlorine, he reached for his dick again, even though it had been less than twelve hours and he wasn't sixteen anymore.

But he was consumed with images of her.

She knocked on the fucking wall. She wants you, you idiot.

He would go to her tonight.

Nicole wasn't used to being this horny when she'd had sex twice in the past twenty-four hours. Last night, then again this morning.

David had heard at least one of those times, hadn't he?

Yet he still wasn't here, and it was three in the afternoon.

She was supposed to be doing chores, but instead she was reclined on the couch, flipping through the options on Netflix and not finding anything that interested her.

Why wasn't he here?

She thought she'd been obvious about what she wanted, but maybe she was still off her game, despite last night.

Or maybe he had stuff to do this afternoon and he'd come here eventually. She pictured him bent over his desk, marking midterms or reviewing lecture notes. Something that required him to wear glasses and furrow his brow in concentration.

Why was that image so intensely hot to her now?

She wondered how he fucked.

Like a husband.

She didn't want a husband. She would hate to be shackled to a man.

When she'd dumped Calvin, it had been so damn *freeing*. She'd found herself again, begun a new phase of her life.

Doubtless, one day David would find someone he wanted to truly be with, like Roy had. But for now, she and David could have some fun. Attentive, husbandly sex sounded appealing—Calvin had never been *attentive*—and he'd probably go down on her a lot. He'd want to get her off and learn what she enjoyed most.

She shifted in her seat.

God, she really wanted to get him into bed, though it was possible he hadn't desired anything more than listening.

But she was pretty sure he did.

~

At nine o'clock that evening, David stood in front of Nicole's door.

He still had doubts, and he was always uncomfortable when

he didn't know exactly where he stood. But he'd been thinking about her all day, and now, here he was.

He finally knocked.

She opened the door a few seconds later, and all he could do was stare.

He'd never seen Nicole dressed up like this before. She was wearing a black off-the-shoulder dress that hugged her body and ended above her knees. Her hair fell in waves down her back.

And she was looking at him like...

He dropped his gaze to the curve of her waist, so clearly outlined in that dress, then checked out her breasts.

"Eyes up here." Her tone was sultry.

David was out of his league, but at the same time, he was starting to feel in his element because he was now very sure where he stood with her. And he loved that she was bold about it.

She pulled him inside and shut the door behind him.

"I was waiting for you," she purred. "Did you hear me last night?"

"Yes." His voice was scratchy. "I heard you."

"You listened, I hope? Now that you have my permission." She placed a single finger to his chest, and the brief touch seared him.

"I did."

There was silence. A charged silence.

"You jerked yourself off?"

He could feel his face turning pink, like it would if he'd dared to drink wine.

"I did," he said.

She touched his cheek. "You're cute."

It was nothing like their dinners together. There was something entirely different between them now.

"I put on this dress just for you. It's even sexier than the one I wore last night, when I picked that guy up at the bar." She shimmied her hips. "What about this morning? Did you hear us then?"

"No, I wasn't home."

"Too bad. I knocked on the wall again afterward."

He swallowed. "What about you? When you were fucking him, were you thinking about me?"

Her eyebrows lifted and she cocked her head.

God, he wanted to kiss her.

And the fact that he seemed to have shocked her...well, it made him feel powerful. Made him want to shock her even more, and also give her all the pleasure that he'd never seen written on her face, only heard.

"Yeah," she said, and her slight pause drove him nuts. "I was thinking about you."

That made David painfully hard.

She pulled down the neckline of her dress, and he got a spectacular view of her plumped up breasts. Had she thought about him kissing those breasts?

When he took a step toward her, it felt like every atom in the room had to adjust its position to accommodate the energy between them.

"What were you thinking about?" He quirked his lips. "Me marking midterms?"

"I do find it hot when you wear glasses."

He immediately thought back to Valentine's Day, when he'd put on glasses to read the menu. He remembered every detail of that day. He'd wondered why she'd struggled to focus on the menu when they sat down, and now, he knew.

She winked at him, and fuck, he wanted her. And she wanted him back, even though he was nothing like the men he'd seen at her apartment.

David wanted her moaning at his touch. He wanted to bring her pleasure after pleasure—more pleasure than he could give her with ube cake or cheese tarts—until she was boneless and giggly.

At last, he closed the distance between them and pressed her against the door. Her breath was coming quicker now. With his hands on her hips, he dropped his head, and she tilted hers up and wrapped her arms around his neck. She was just a few inches shorter than him, and her body felt soft and perfect against his.

"Nicole," he whispered, a part of him still struggling to believe this was real.

And then he kissed her.

It was somehow needy but gentle—he didn't know how else to describe it.

Electrifying, too.

Her mouth was hot. She tasted faintly of chocolate, and he wondered if there was another man who brought her desserts, too—he didn't like the thought.

He kissed her harder, then he slid his mouth down her neck. She arched, just as he'd imagined she'd do, and released a breathy sigh.

All he wanted was to hear her make more sounds like that.

For him.

He spun her around so her back was to his chest, and as he continued kissing her neck, he pressed his erection against her ass.

"David," she moaned.

Hearing her say his name was pretty wonderful.

"What do you want from me tonight?" he asked.

"Anything you want to give me."

Oh, God. He had so many ideas.

"But don't handcuff me or tie me up," she said. "I don't do that."

It didn't surprise him. Nicole would never want to be completely restrained and at the mercy of someone else.

She reached back and cupped his cock through his pants. When he nearly stumbled, she winked at him again. She was still far too cheeky.

He lifted up the bottom of her skirt, all the way to her hips, so her ass was mostly bare—she wore a little black thong.

He closed his eyes and hissed out a breath.

And then he slipped a finger inside her.

11

NICOLE HAD BEEN WAITING all day for David to touch her, and he was finally doing it. He pumped his finger in and out of her before trailing his wet hand up and down her thigh.

He was such a tease.

His breath was hot on her neck, and his erection was still against her ass. There was something thrilling about making this man hard, about him jerking off because she was having sex next door. Maybe she'd been wrong about her type…

But she couldn't follow that thread of thought, not when his hands were all over her.

"You know what I want to do?" he murmured.

She didn't think he'd say anything more after that, but she was wrong.

"I want to fuck you with my fingers," he said. "Suck you and lick you all over. I bet you have lots of toys."

"Toys," she repeated.

"Yes. Dildos and vibrators and such. I think you have a very demanding pussy."

She looked back at him. He was turning red again, but fuck, he'd still said those words.

David Cho, swearing and talking dirty to her.

The first time she'd laid eyes on him, she'd never imagined such a thing was possible. What sort of filthy thoughts had filled his mind when he heard her through the wall?

She liked that he understood she just really loved sex; he didn't think she was suffering from low self-esteem and that was why she craved sexual attention.

"When you're not with someone else," he said, "you're an expert at taking care of your own needs, aren't you?"

"Yes." She rolled her hips back against him.

"But tonight, I want to be the one who uses all of those toys on you."

"You're ambitious." She tried for a light tone, but it was difficult when she couldn't help thinking of lying spread-eagle on her bed as he examined the large collection in her night table.

"I try my best." He slid her thong down her legs, then pulled her dress over her head. Her bra hit the ground a second later. "Very nice."

He turned her around and kissed her lips, and then he dipped his head to her breasts, sucking one nipple into his mouth as he slid his hand between her legs again, parting her folds to thrust a finger inside.

She was naked, and he was still fully clothed.

He dropped to his knees and put his mouth on her, and even though she'd expected it, she still cried out in shock. The warm pressure of his mouth was just so *good*.

His pussy-licking skills turned out to be exceptional—and she would know. Nicole had been eaten out by lots of men. And while David closed his eyes and was clearly enjoying himself, she also had the impression that he was studiously paying attention to what she liked so he could ace the exam later.

She shoved her fingers into his hair and pressed his head firmly against her. He laughed softly at her greediness.

"Come on, David," she moaned. "Make me come."

At those words, he pushed two fingers inside her and sucked her clit, and she came apart, bucking against his face as he licked her through her climax.

Her legs were a little shaky as he led her to the bedroom and set her down on the bed.

"Now show me what you have," he said.

She cupped her breasts in her hands and flicked her nipples.

He laughed again, that soft, sexy laugh, but then he switched to a commanding tone that made her shiver.

"You know what I mean," he said sternly.

Oh dear God, he was good at this.

She reached into her bedside table and tossed a bunch of things on the bed. Two strips of condoms. Lube. A vibrator. Two dildos. Another vibrator. Another dildo. An anal plug.

"You like toys?" she asked him.

"Anything and everything I can use to make you feel good."

Her inner muscles clenched. Unfortunately, there was nothing for them to clench around.

He picked up a thick dildo. "I hope you'll think of me the next time you use these on yourself."

She inhaled swiftly. Jesus, he was surprising her. This wasn't at all how she'd expected this encounter to go. She was losing some of the control she'd thought she'd have with him, but she couldn't say she was complaining.

Although she was going to complain if he didn't start using the toy in his hand.

"Come on. I'm ready." She licked her finger and ran it along her inner lips.

He set down the dildo. "I don't think you're ready for that one yet."

For fuck's sake.

He picked up a different dildo.

"Be careful with that one," she said lightly. "It's handblown glass."

This was apparently the wrong thing to say, because he made a show of studying it carefully, running his fingers along the ridges and delaying her gratification even further. It was a glass candy cane; the ridges were red.

"Very festive," he said.

"A little Christmas gift to myself."

He drizzled some lube on it, then ran the tip over her entrance. She moaned.

"It's nice to see you and touch you when you moan like that," he said.

"Rather than listening on the other side of the...ahhh."

He'd shoved it all the way inside her, and he chuckled at her reaction. She tried to rearrange her brain so it would think of a snarky comeback, but then his lips were on hers as he moved the toy in and out.

"Do you need clitoral stimulation to come?" he asked.

"No, but—"

"Guess I won't use a vibrator, then."

"Oh, fuck you."

She clawed at him, and he just laughed again.

"You're wearing too many clothes," she whined.

"All in good time."

He continued to kiss her as he sped up his pace with the candy cane dildo, and she squirmed around the hard toy and thought of his dick, making a tent in his trousers.

And then he bit her shoulder as he thrust the toy in hard, and she cried out, her orgasm washing over her unexpectedly.

When she was alone, one or two orgasms were always enough, but with him, she was nowhere close to done. What was he going to do next?

He left the dildo inside her. "What's the greatest number of times you've come in a night?"

Nicole was lucky—she'd always orgasmed easily.

"Eleven," she said, trying to sound flippant, but she couldn't.

"Very well, twelve it is."

"David!"

"You can do it," he said. "I believe in you."

He picked up a small wand-shaped vibrator, turned it on, and pressed it to her clit.

She immediately jerked her hips.

"I could do this for hours." He lay down on his side, his head propped up on his hand, as he pleasured her.

She was so sensitive. Why was she so sensitive with him?

Yet it still wasn't enough.

Nicole wasn't shy in bed, so she gripped the curve of the candy cane and started sliding it in and out of her pussy.

"Yes, that's pretty." He slid down her body and turned off the vibrator.

She barely had a chance to protest before his tongue took its place.

She jerked again and cried out.

"I would have heard that from my bedroom." He picked up her anal plug. "Will you let me use this on you?"

When she nodded, he rolled her onto her stomach, then lubed up his finger and pressed it into her ass. This was closely followed by the anal plug. She hadn't used it in a while, and it took her body a moment to accept it.

"Good job," he murmured, kissing the side of her face.

She felt like a doll that he was using for his pleasure, except it was really all about her pleasure, wasn't it?

He slid the dildo in and out of her a few times before removing it, but it was immediately replaced with her thickest, longest dildo.

She gasped when it was seated fully inside her, and with the plug... God, she was full.

"David."

He lay down on top of her. He didn't move either of the toys, just kissed her neck.

"You're so greedy," he said admiringly before he started pounding her with the dildo.

It didn't take long before she was biting the pillow to muffle her scream, and then he gave her only a moment's rest before he started moving it inside her again. This time, he added an egg-shaped vibrator.

It was an overload of sensation. Using toys by herself never felt this way.

And he was right. She would think of him when she used the toys in the future.

She came once more, and it was all starting to blur together. Her senses were heightened. She was in this weird state where she felt like she was constantly on the verge of orgasm. It was almost painful to be this aroused, and her brain was incapable of coherent thought, and yet...

"Do you want me to stop?" he asked.

"No!"

He laughed, and she couldn't even muster up the tiniest bit of outrage. Instead, she let out an unhinged giggle.

Nicole knew all about amazing sex, but somehow, it had never been quite like this.

Except for one problem.

"David, I want your cock inside me."

"Not yet."

Not yet. She would trust that he'd give it to her eventually. His devotion to her pleasure was intoxicating, even if he didn't let her have any say in it.

He put aside the vibrator and fucked her hard with the dildo, and she came again and laughed afterward, even though she didn't usually laugh when she came.

Her orgasms were no longer as intense, but still, she could think of nothing else.

"David," she moaned.

On and on, he pleasured her with her toys. She was a blubbering mess, practically sobbing and laughing at the same time.

"Twelve," he said.

She'd completely lost track, but he'd been counting, of course.

When she heard him rip open a foil packet, she whimpered.

"Just a moment," he said, running his hand soothingly up and down her back. "I'll be inside you in just a moment."

She buried her head in the pillow, and then his cock brushed her entrance.

"Please." She didn't care how desperate she sounded.

As he started to push inside, she cried out and clutched the pillow.

He was still clothed. She wanted to protest, but that would involve stringing multiple words together, and she couldn't do that right now.

He stayed motionless. "You feel incredible. I won't last long."

He fucked her with slow, deep strokes as he pressed kisses up and down her neck, her cheek, her shoulders. She felt him in every cell in her body.

With one particularly deep stroke, she was almost there. Then he touched her sensitized clit, and she was gone, and he was gone, too.

Lucky thirteen.

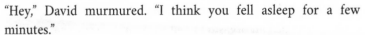

"Hey," David murmured. "I think you fell asleep for a few minutes."

"Mmmm."

He was sitting beside her on the bed, fully dressed. Nicole hadn't gotten to see him at *all*. That was supremely unfair.

"I ran you a bath," he said.

"Are you going to join me?"

"No, I'll wash your toys."

She made a sound of protest, but that was nice of him.

He led her to the bathroom and helped her into the tub. It was full of bubbles, and they amused her more than they should.

"I think you need to wear your glasses to clean," she mumbled.

"I don't have them with me." He quirked his lips, then rolled up his sleeves and started washing.

It felt like a very domestic scene. They were in the washroom together, but not because they were having sex in the shower, which was the only thing she ever did in the washroom with a man.

He set her handblown glass dildo on a towel.

Yes, very domestic.

She giggled.

He raised his eyebrows, but she said nothing, and he didn't insist on an explanation.

Nicole reclined in the tub with her eyes closed. Though she felt a bit dopey, at the same time, she was overly aware of the warm water on her skin, the mild scent of the bath foam, the quiet sounds of David washing her toys.

He helped her out of the bathtub and dried her off—nobody had dried her off in a long time. He wrapped the towel around her and led her to the kitchen, where he poured her a glass of water.

"I'm going to leave now," he said. "Make sure you lock the door, okay?"

"I know how to lock a door." She stuck out her bottom lip.

"When you're in post-orgasmic bliss?"

"I haven't had an orgasm in half an hour. You sure have a high opinion of the orgasms you give."

He leaned in to kiss her forehead.

There was something about the kiss that pierced the "post-orgasmic bliss" she was feeling, just a little.

He was gentle. Taking care of her after it was over.

She still felt rather boneless, but not quite like before.

"I'll see you Friday?" she said.

He hesitated. "Friday."

And then he was gone and she couldn't help giggling again before collapsing in bed.

12

BEEP. Beep. Beep.

Sleepily, Nicole reached out and hit the snooze button on her alarm.

Beep. Beep. Beep.

Why was it still going off? Had she missed the button in her groggy state?

She pushed it again, and the noise mercifully stopped.

She sighed and stretched to one side then the other, pointing her toes. Now that her annoyance with her blasted alarm clock was fading, she felt...good.

Yesterday, she'd had sex with two men, and her body was a little sore but sated. It had been a fun day.

What was David doing on the other side of the wall? Was he awake yet? Making coffee? Picking out a professorly sweater for the day?

The fact that he could be in his bedroom, so close to her...

Nicole suddenly sat up. What if he slept nude? What if he'd just come out of the shower? What had his walls seen that she hadn't?

Last night had been different from what she'd anticipated.

She'd expected to enjoy sex with David—she wouldn't have slept with him otherwise—but she hadn't expected him to make her practically drunk with orgasms. She hadn't expected their playful banter. The way he'd fucked her with so many different toys...

She needed something inside her again.

She jerked open her night table drawer, but a couple of her dildos were missing.

Right. She remembered now.

Nicole padded to the bathroom and returned to bed with all her clean toys. She put most of them away but kept out a vibrator and the candy cane dildo, which she slowly slid inside her.

Yes.

She'd gotten off many times only eight hours ago, but Nicole had always had a high sex drive, and the idea that David could be stroking himself, just on the other side of this wall—well, that made her squirm.

It wasn't long before she was shuddering and moaning into her pillow. She couldn't afford a long masturbation session when she had to go to work.

But she did knock on the wall, just in case David was there.

Then she regretted it. What if he was still asleep? She wanted him to get his beauty rest.

And next time, she was determined to actually see him—all of him. Maybe tonight...

Except she'd told him that she'd see him on Friday, and it was probably for the best. She didn't want to get in the habit of seeing him every day.

This was an excellent development, though.

A sex partner next door was just what she needed.

"I want to try an experiment." Murray leaned against David's desk.

David tried not to groan. He had an inbox full of emails—why were there so many emails?—and a grant application to submit, and he hadn't been able to think clearly all morning because apparently he'd lost his brain in Nicole's bedroom.

"An experiment?" he asked.

"Where's your phone?"

David took out his phone.

"Okay," Murray said. "Now send me a text message."

"What should it say?"

"Anything," Murray said impatiently. "The details aren't important."

David sent a single-word text: *Hello*.

Murray pulled his phone out of his pocket and turned it on. "I got your message. It's very boring, though."

"You told me the details weren't important."

"Experiment complete."

"What was the experiment?"

"To see if I'd still receive a text message that had been sent when my phone was off."

David frowned. "Of course you would. But you don't keep your phone turned on?"

"Why would I?"

Although Murray was a scientist who'd been using email for decades and was quite good with certain aspects of technology, things like smartphones and social media were foreign to him. In fact, David was surprised his colleague even had a smartphone.

"You Millennials." Murray shook his head. "There was some other reason I came here...ah, yes! To remind you of the alumni dinner this Friday."

When Murray left to go to his lecture, David banged his head against his desk.

He was supposed to see Nicole on Friday. He'd been researching which dessert to get her, and possibly also fantasizing about what they'd do together in bed.

And he couldn't help wondering what she wanted.

His impression was that Nicole had a variety of bedmates. Did she ever have relationships with them? Or did she avoid relationships, for one reason or another?

It was rare for David to have sex outside of a relationship; in fact, it didn't usually interest him. But he desperately wanted to be in Nicole's bed.

And to be there more than once.

That, perhaps, was part of the reason he'd acted the way he had yesterday. He hadn't taken off his clothes or let her ride him —he suspected Nicole enjoyed being on top—because he'd wanted there to be new things for them to do together, hoping that would make her desire another night with him.

From the way she'd said, "I'll see you Friday?" it sounded like she was thinking of being in bed together, too, but she hadn't mentioned seeing him before that, to his disappointment.

Now Friday wouldn't happen because of the alumni dinner. When would he see her next?

He briefly wondered if he should have asked to stay the night, but he'd had a few reasons for not asking. For starters, he'd worried that she'd regret it. Not the sex itself, but maybe she would have regretted letting him stay overnight when it was so easy for him to return home.

David cursed the alumni dinner—although he usually didn't mind it—and sent Nicole a text, letting her know that he wouldn't be able to see her this Friday.

"And if you are losing an argument," Po Po said on screen, "create a, how do you say it? Diversion. Pretend you see snake or cockroach! Trust me, most people will freak out because they are weaklings. Or pretend to faint. Like this." She executed her fake faint. "This works better if you are old. Then everyone will be so thankful you are alive, and they will forget you are losing argument. Good trick."

When the video ended, Nicole put down her phone and looked at her sibling.

"Uh, Cam," Nicole said. "Remember Christmas, the year Kelsey was applying to universities, and Po Po didn't like her choices and—"

"She fainted," Cam said, using air quotes. "Do you think—"

"Yeah, I most definitely think."

They burst into laughter right as the waiter arrived with their moussaka. The two of them were having Saturday lunch at a Greek restaurant that Nicole had never been to before, but she'd eaten the food when David had gotten it for takeout.

She felt slightly disappointed that she hadn't seen him yesterday. At least, she told herself it was no more than *slight* disappointment.

"Did you see the one about online shopping?" Cam asked.

Nicole shook her head, then located the video.

On screen, Po Po was sitting in front of the computer. "Wah, why would I do online shopping? You cannot argue about the price! This is a terrible idea."

Nicole chuckled as she tucked her phone into her purse and dug into her moussaka.

It was just as good as she remembered.

"So," Cam said, "any big plans for tonight?"

"My friends and I are going to the lounge at L."

"The place that's so fancy its name is a single letter?"

"Exactly."

"It sounds…how do I say this? Pretty fucking pretentious. Not your choice, was it?"

"No, one of my friends is dating…" Nicole paused. "I'm not sure I should say. Oh, whatever. Just don't tell anyone. One of my friends is dating Colton Sanders."

Cam's eyebrows shot up. "*The* Colton Sanders?"

"That was my reaction."

"Must be Sierra. Charlotte has a boyfriend, and I don't see Rose dating someone like that."

"You're correct."

Cam made a face. "I bet he's a pompous ass who's used to having everything handed to him on a silver platter. Not that you should tell him that, but…"

"I'll reserve judgement. For now."

"So that's why you're so happy today?" Cam asked. "Because you're looking forward to going to this lounge?"

"No! I mean…" The truth was, Nicole had made plans to see David tomorrow evening. That was what she was looking forward to more than anything.

She didn't usually lie to her sibling, and Cam—unlike Mom and Po Po—didn't give Nicole a hard time over things. But Cam was newly in a relationship and would probably read something romantic into Nicole fucking her neighbor, even though there was nothing romantic about it.

"Just glad to see you, and I'm excited to hang out with my friends," Nicole said. "And to do something different."

Cam raised an eyebrow but didn't say anything.

"Seriously," Nicole said, then wondered if her insistence was suspicious.

Maybe it was, but whatever.

It was only natural to look forward to good sex, wasn't it?

13

NICOLE SWAYED her hips as she walked from the subway to L.

She was feeling pretty damn sexy tonight.

After lunch with Cam, the two of them had gone on an unplanned shopping trip. Cam had gotten a vest, a tie, and a pair of earrings; Nicole had bought a red dress, which she was wearing now. She was also wearing the shoes with an ankle strap that she'd bought on her shopping trip with Charlotte.

The nice thing about L was that it was closer to home than Ossington Cider Bar—only a single subway line, followed by a short walk. Still, Nicole was late. She was supposed to be there half an hour ago, but she'd spent quite a bit of time primping. She felt like she ought to look particularly good tonight since she was going to a fancy place and meeting new people, plus she just enjoyed looking hot.

To her distress, she kept wondering what David would think of this outfit, kept imagining him slowly unzipping the side of the dress... He was on her mind a little more than she'd like.

Her libido had been in overdrive all week, and maybe tonight she'd meet some rich dude in a suit with a penthouse nearby—she wasn't sure she wanted to wait for tomorrow.

An East Asian man with long hair, tied back in a ponytail, held open the door to L for her. She tilted her head and gave him a seductive smile, and she knew she already had him eating out of her hand.

Oh, yes, she was in good form.

"I'm meeting Colton Sanders's party," she told the hostess.

"Right this way," the hostess said, leading Nicole toward the back of the dimly-lit lounge.

Sierra, Rose, Amy, and Charlotte were seated on a cluster of chairs that looked very cool and dreadfully uncomfortable. There was a long table with drinks and food.

"Nicole!" Rose bounced up and threw her arms around Nicole.

Nicole hadn't been prepared for the ambush and nearly fell backward on her new heels.

She met Sierra's eyes. "What's she been drinking?"

Rose didn't usually greet people with such an enthusiastic hug...unless she was drunk.

"I don't even know what it is!" Rose dragged Nicole toward a chair. "But it's soooo good."

"I'm drinking a dark chocolate espresso and orange martini." Charlotte lifted her glass. She was wearing jeans and a blazer, but everyone else was wearing a dress.

The waiter came around, and Nicole asked for a martini like Charlotte's.

"Ooh, let me explain all the food to you," Rose said.

"Yes!" Amy said. "Colton got us this very fancy charcuterie board."

"Where's Colton?" Nicole asked Sierra.

"Oh, he's around," Sierra said. "He saw someone he wanted to talk to, but he'll be back."

"This," Rose pointed out a cheese, "is made with actual gold leaf. And this prosciutto is the best I've ever tasted. I nearly orgasmed when I had it." She covered her mouth. "Shit, did I say that out loud?"

"Okay, that's it," Charlotte said. "You're cut off."

"But I can still eat the cheese pooped by monkeys, right?" Rose asked.

"No, that's not the cheese you like. It's the sheep's cheese."

"Ooh, right! I love sheep! So fluffy and cuddly. I got a sheep plushie, did I tell you?"

"Wait a second." Nicole reached for some prosciutto, a little afraid of the cheese situation. "One of the cheeses was pooped by monkeys?"

"No, Rose is confused," Charlotte said. "But they have civet coffee—you know what that is? It's really expensive. Coffee cherries are eaten by civets, not monkeys, then the partially digested coffee beans are collected from their poop. Everyone wanted me to order it."

"Hey, don't blame this on me! I said no such thing." Sierra crossed her arms. "There are concerns about how the civets are treated."

Nicole had tried many weird things. Bird's nest soup, for example, was made of hardened bird saliva. But she'd pass on civet coffee.

"This cheese," Amy said, pointing to another one, "is made from the milk of some special type of llama."

"You guys are so drunk," Charlotte muttered. "It's from a special kind of donkey."

"Same thing!" Rose giggled.

"No, a llama and a donkey are not the same animal. Do you need to go back to kindergarten?"

Nicole felt like she should have gotten here earlier.

She helped herself to a piece of bread that was no doubt very posh and expensive, along with some of the sheep's cheese—she'd always loved sheep's cheese.

She groaned as she chewed. God, this was the best sheep's

cheese she'd ever had. The bread was also very good, but not worth the extortionate price that was likely charged for it.

"Isn't it amazing?" Rose asked.

Nicole was about to answer when the server returned and handed her a martini. He also set down a selection of ramekins with what looked like chocolate mousse and crème brûlée. Colton had yet to make an appearance, but apparently he'd ordered these for them.

The chocolate mousse was incredibly decadent and not overly sweet, with a bite of raspberry curd in the middle. Nicole could eat this forever.

She felt a moment of guilt for eating all these expensive foods and drinks that she wasn't paying for, but then she reminded herself that Colton was a billionaire, and fuck it, he could afford to spend money on his girlfriend's friends.

Though where on earth was he?

"Is that a new dress?" Amy asked Nicole. "I love it."

"Thank you. Yours is beautiful, too."

Amy's dress was also red, but rather than a skirt that hugged her thighs, it was flouncy and ended just below her knees.

Rose nudged Nicole. "That guy is looking at you." She pointed to the right, not at all subtly.

Nicole looked up, locking eyes with a man who had an uncanny resemblance to Jason Momoa.

Her first thought was, *Wow, Po Po would be impressed.*

In fact, Po Po would probably find this whole place a hoot.

A laugh escaped Nicole's lips, and then she wondered what the hell was wrong with her. Normally, if a guy like that was undressing her with his eyes, she'd be strutting over to him, but for some reason, she didn't feel like it.

"You're not going?" Sierra asked.

"Nah," Nicole said. "My grandmother calling Jason Momoa 'hunky' on TikTok has kind of ruined my interest."

Charlotte looked suspicious but remained silent.

Nicole ate more cheese and drank her delicious drink. She'd been worried this place would be all about the aesthetic and the food would be disappointing, but it was very good. Or maybe some of this stuff was special at Colton's request, because he was Colton fucking Sanders.

Just then, the man who'd held the door open for her walked by, and she was about to tilt her head and wink at him, then decided she wasn't in the mood.

Flirting was just so much *effort*.

She'd thought she might take a guy home, and David would listen from the other side of the wall. Then tomorrow, she'd go to him.

But she was starting to like the idea of just having sex with David tonight.

She sent him a text. *Any plans for the evening?*

Then she slipped her phone into her purse and helped herself to another chocolate mousse. More than five had been brought to the table, so she didn't feel guilty.

"You okay?" Amy asked her. "You're a little quiet."

Nicole shook her head. "I'm fine."

"There are lots of hot guys here, aren't there?" Amy waggled her eyebrows.

"Hey, you're a married woman."

"Not for me. For you, of course!"

"We'll see."

"Or for you." Amy turned to Rose.

Rose giggled. "You want *me* to go home with a guy?"

"No, you've had too much to drink. But you could get his number."

Rose found this hilarious. Nicole wasn't sure if this was because Rose was drunk, or because she found the idea of a guy being interested in her ridiculous. The latter made Nicole sad, especially since she knew Rose wanted marriage and happily ever after, and she wanted her friend to have it.

Nicole finished her martini and asked the server for another one, just as her phone vibrated in her purse.

She smiled. "I'll be back," she said to her friends. "I'm going to the washroom."

She walked away before anyone could offer to go with her.

I'm at home watching Netflix, David's text read.

I'm out at a fancy lounge with some friends, Nicole replied.

Having a good time?

She pushed open the door to the washroom, then started typing.

Wearing a sexy new red dress. Thought of you when I bought it today. I bet you'd like it.

Somehow, the image of David at home, stretched out on his couch, reading her text... God, why did that turn her on so much?

It was partly the contrast that was doing it for her. He was normally calm and sweet and mild-mannered, yet he'd fucked her so hard with her toys. There was something particularly delicious about knowing he could be like that. And it had only been their first time together.

Dammit. There were other men here, and all she could do was anxiously wait for his text.

Show me a picture? he said.

She re-applied her lipstick, then snapped a picture of herself in the mirror. She sent it to him. *You wanna fuck me?*

His answer was almost immediate. *How could I not?*

She squeezed her thighs together.

She wondered if David had ever done much sexting. If he was blushing in his living room right now. She kind of wanted to push and see what he would send her, but decided against it.

Can I come over when I get home? In two hours? I don't want to wait until tomorrow.

"You okay? What are you doing in here?"

"Ahhh!" Nicole shrieked.

Charlotte frowned. "You don't usually startle so easily. I just came to check up on you. You've been gone a while, and you weren't flirting with the guy who looks like Jason Momoa. You sure everything's okay?"

Nicole tried to get control of herself. "Just arranging a booty call."

Why did she sound guilty? There was no reason to sound guilty. She never felt guilty about enjoying sex.

Charlotte regarded her suspiciously. "Do you *like* someone, Nicole? Is it David?"

"I just enjoy having sex with him, that's all. He gave me a record number of orgasms last Sunday."

"So you *are* sleeping with him now."

Nicole's phone vibrated.

Sounds good, his message read. *Now here's a little something to get you excited.*

OMG, was he going to send her a picture of his dick? She didn't actually know what his dick looked like; she only knew how it felt inside her.

But surely David wouldn't send her a dick pic?

The photo came through a few seconds later.

It was simply a picture of his glasses resting on a table, and she laughed.

Charlotte grabbed the phone. "He sent you a picture of his glasses?"

Nicole shrugged. "I told him that I like how he looks in glasses."

"Can't wait to show this to everyone."

"No! It'll make them think I have a crush on him, and it's not like that, I promise."

"You owe me for my silence," Charlotte muttered. "A hundred bucks."

"Is blackmail your new hobby?"

"Just kidding. I'll keep my mouth shut. For now."

They returned to the rest of their friends. Nicole's drink was waiting for her, and she took a healthy swallow.

"Colton still isn't here?" she asked, trying to sound casual, like she wasn't thinking of what awaited her at home.

Sierra sighed. "Let me text him again."

Fifteen minutes later, Colton still hadn't appeared, but a plate of oysters was placed on their table. Nicole couldn't help wishing that she could sexily eat oysters in front of David.

Stop thinking about him! You'll see him soon.

"Oysters!" Amy said. "You know, I only tried them for the first time last year. I bet these are more expensive, though." She ate one. "Oh, yes, they're very good, not that I'm a connoisseur or anything."

Nicole helped herself to an oyster.

And then she finally saw him.

Colton Sanders—she recognized him from the news—smoothly walked toward them, a charming smile on his face. His gaze was on Sierra, but then it flitted over to Nicole, and there was something about the way he looked at her...

No, Nicole must be imagining it.

Colton was now back to looking at Sierra as though she was the center of his universe.

Yet there was something about the man that seemed a little artificial.

"Hello, ladies," he said. "Enjoying yourselves?"

Rose tittered. "Yes!"

"The food is excellent," Nicole said. "I'm glad you could finally grace us with your presence." She tried not to sound snarky and thought she succeeded.

"Yes, well," he said. "Duty calls sometimes, but now I'm yours for the rest of the night."

And with that, a bottle of champagne appeared at their table.

Colton picked Sierra up from her chair, sat down, and settled her in his lap as the server poured champagne for each of them.

Nicole enjoyed good food and drink, and it was fun to see her friends, but dammit, she kept thinking of that photo of David's glasses. She wished she could take some of this delicious food home to him.

Well, why not?

When the server came around, she asked for a chocolate mousse to go and told him to put it on a separate bill. If it was a little expensive, that was fine. She hadn't paid for anything else, and it wasn't like it would be as expensive as gold leaf cheese or civet coffee.

She sipped her champagne and thought about what she'd do with David tonight.

She would *not* let him have all the control.

In fact...

She grinned as she thought of a certain item in the bottom drawer of her night table. Something David hadn't found last weekend. Amy had discovered a box of these in her great aunt's house, and Nicole had been happy to take a few.

"What are you smiling at, Nicole?" Sierra asked.

"Oh, just thinking about the man I've got waiting for me." Hopefully her friends wouldn't think this was anything more than a booty call.

Because it *wasn't* anything more, even if Charlotte seemed doubtful.

Nicole said her goodbyes and hugged her friends.

"Nice to meet you, Colton," she said.

"You, too, Nicole." He held her hand for just a second too long.

But she didn't give that too much thought.

She was going to get laid.

14

DAVID TURNED OFF THE TELEVISION. Nicole had texted him twenty minutes ago to say she was coming home now, so he didn't have time to watch another episode. Instead, he put on his glasses and picked up the book he was reading, but he couldn't concentrate.

They'd originally made plans for tomorrow, and he'd spent today wondering if he would hear her having sex with someone else tonight. The idea turned him on yet made him uncomfortable at the same time.

And then she'd started texting him.

Speaking of...

His phone buzzed.

Come on over, she said.

When he knocked on her door, she immediately opened it and gave him a saucy smile. He slipped off his shoes—perhaps it was stupid to wear shoes to go right next door, but he'd done it anyway—and drank her in.

She was wearing the red dress she'd sent him a picture of earlier, and it was breathtaking.

"Like what you see?" Her tone suggested she knew exactly how much he liked it.

But could she really know just how much? It seemed impossible.

Before he knew what was happening, she'd pushed him against the wall and stuck her tongue down his throat. He was happy to surrender as she rolled her body against his. Like some kind of fantasy come to life, but she was utterly real.

"You did something very naughty last time," she said.

"Did I?" he murmured. "All those toys I stuck in your pussy?"

This appeared to shock her, which he enjoyed.

They were different together when they were fucking or about to fuck. They bantered in a way they didn't otherwise, although maybe sharing a meal with her would be different now that they were having sex.

She tapped his chest with one finger. "The problem was that you didn't get naked."

As she started unbuttoning his shirt, he felt a little self-conscious. He didn't look like the more muscled guys she'd brought home in the past.

But there was zero disappointment in her expression as she reached the bottom button and pushed the sides of his shirt apart.

"Mmmm." She winked at him as she dropped his shirt to the floor and started on his belt.

He'd been wearing pajama pants earlier, but when she'd told him she was coming over, wearing that dress, he'd figured he ought to make more of an effort.

His belt hit the ground, followed by his pants, and he stood there in only his boxers.

"Much better," she purred.

She pressed herself against him and started ravishing him with her kisses. She tasted of chocolate and coffee, with a slightly salty tang, and the unexpected combination was perfect right now. *She* brought it all together.

He growled as he felt around her dress and finally happened

upon the zipper. He started sliding it down, but she stepped back and shook her finger at him.

"Uh-uh," she said. "Not yet. You got me naked when you were completely clothed last time, so it's only fair if I do the reverse today."

"You're making this about fairness? I thought you played dirty."

She laughed. It wasn't a husky, sexual laugh, just one of unexpected delight.

Which also made him hard.

"Come to the bedroom," she said.

He followed her, and she gestured for him to lie back on the bed. She opened the bottom drawer of her night table and pulled out two pairs of furry pink handcuffs.

"I don't like handcuffs on myself," she said, "but can I use them on you?"

He nodded. "Just don't leave me restrained for an hour. I don't want to be too sore tomorrow."

"No? I was sore on Monday and it was quite nice. I got myself off again that morning and wondered what you were doing on the other side of the wall."

Fuck, this woman drove him mad.

And somehow, he seemed to have pleased her last weekend.

"Don't worry," she said as she fastened his wrists to the headboard. "I won't leave you here for too long, I promise."

She started strutting around the room. His gaze was fixed on her, and she clearly loved the attention. At the base of the bed, she turned away from him, bent over, and slid down her panties, which she left on the floor.

Then she crawled up the bed, a predatory look in her eyes. She sat down on top of him, and he growled again.

"Yeah, you like that?" she asked, grinding her hips against him.

Oh, God. He wanted to be inside her so badly.

She slid farther up his body, hiking up her dress at the same time, and now he could feel her wetness on his chest.

"I think it's time for me to see you naked." She pulled off his boxers and tossed them to the side. Her gaze was riveted on his crotch. "Yes, very nice."

He rather wanted to puff up his chest.

She bent over, giving him an excellent view of her cleavage—surely not an accident—as she wrapped her hand around his cock.

He made a strangled sound.

She smiled at him, then took him in her mouth.

He made more incoherent sounds.

It had been a very long time since he'd received a blowjob, and oh, she was good, which was no surprise. If she didn't let up, this would end far too soon.

But Nicole, of course, knew exactly what she was doing. She released him with a *pop*, then reached over to get something out of the night table.

The candy cane dildo.

She held it up to his lips, and he took it in his mouth. Once he'd gotten it wet, she came up on her knees and slid it inside herself.

He tried to reach out and touch her but quickly happened upon resistance.

The handcuffs. Right.

Nicole kept her gaze on him as she slid the toy in and out of her pussy.

"You want a taste?" she asked.

He nodded, expecting her to sit on his face, but she removed the toy and held it to his mouth again. He licked her juices off it.

"Now I've got something else for you to taste." She reached over to the bedside table and picked up a plastic container he hadn't noticed before, because he'd been entirely focused on her. It looked like chocolate something or other. "I had two of these tonight. But I'm used to eating dessert with you these days, and I wished I could eat it with you."

That comment struck him a bit differently than everything else she'd said, and it took a hold of his heart. Before he could reflect on that, she was holding a spoon up to his mouth.

"Chocolate mousse," she said. "Isn't it good?"

"Yes." It was good. Very good.

She fed him another bite. This one had a surprising burst of something tangy and fruity.

"Raspberry curd," she told him.

He was salivating at the thought of the next bite, but she put it in her mouth instead, giving him a coy little smile, then making a noise very similar to the ones she made when she orgasmed.

God, he loved how much she was enjoying this, but he made a sound of frustration. She wasn't feeding him. She wasn't touching his cock. She was still mostly dressed...and she'd put the toy back inside her and he couldn't touch it.

After setting the mousse back on the table, she reclined partially and shifted her dress up farther. She moved the toy in and out of her body, using the curve of the candy cane as a handle. Her eyes flew closed. She started moaning, and then she trembled, and he groaned as though he was the one who'd come.

He was painfully hard.

She set the toy aside and slid up his body, pressing her crotch to his mouth. He licked her avidly, but it wasn't long before she dismounted and got something out of her night table again.

A condom.

"Thank God," he muttered, and she laughed.

She rolled it on and sat on his cock.

He squeezed his eyes shut and pulled at the restraints.

She felt fantastic.

He opened his eyes because he didn't want to miss the sight of her riding him, and indeed, it was spectacular. As she bounced on his dick, she unzipped her dress and pulled it over her head, never missing a beat, then tossed her bra to the side. She cupped her breasts in her hands and stroked her nipples with her thumbs, tipping her head back as she did so. When he jerked his hips upward, she came, and the orgasm seemed to catch her off guard, which he found rather gratifying.

She bent over to kiss his lips, her bare chest against his for the first time, and it was too much for him.

She swallowed his cry of pleasure before dismounting and removing the handcuffs.

~

"Would you even be capable of walking home right now?" Nicole asked.

They were both still naked, curled up on their sides, facing each other.

"I live right next door," David said.

"Oh, I know."

This woman. He couldn't get enough of her.

"You're welcome to stay, if you like," she said. "I don't mind."

"You don't mind," he repeated. "But what do you *want*?"

She walked her fingertips up his chest. "I'd like you to stay. That way we can have sex first thing in the morning."

It didn't seem to be all about sex, though, because she immediately snuggled up to him. He couldn't help feeling affection for her that was completely separate from their friendship. He stroked his hand up and down her back, now that he was able to move his arms again.

But though she clearly enjoyed being with him and fucking him, he still had no idea where he stood with her.

Other thoughts were floating around in his brain, but it was hard to grasp them. He wasn't usually awake at one in the morning, nor was he usually in bed with a gorgeous woman.

But one thought did manage to take hold.

"Nicole," he said, "we didn't finish the chocolate mousse, did we?"

She immediately sat up. "No, we didn't. We'd better finish it now. Letting that go to waste would be a travesty."

Yes, she made him smile.

[15]

When Nicole woke up on Sunday, someone was stirring beside her.

Grinning, she wrapped an arm around David, who was lying on his side and looking at her alarm clock.

"Good morning," she murmured, kissing his cheek. "You have anywhere to be?"

"I usually go swimming on Sunday morning."

Ah. He must have been coming back from the pool the morning she first saw him, when he was carrying a duffel bag.

She hid her disappointment. If he wanted to go to the pool, she wouldn't stop him.

He rolled over. "But I can skip it today."

"Mmm, I'd like that," she said, moving on top of him.

They were both still naked, and she moaned as she felt his skin against hers, his hardening length against her thigh.

He smiled up at her. "I have a request."

"Yes?"

"No handcuffs this time. I want to touch you."

He slid his hands up her chest, brushing a thumb over her nipple. Then he brushed her lower lip, continuing to smile at her.

She could feel herself slowly returning his smile, and the next thing she knew, she was on her back and he was above her.

She laughed and sank into the mattress as he kissed and licked her all over.

Nicole may have eaten expensive oysters and cheese last night, but this...this was luxury. Waking up with a beautiful naked man who was intent on pleasuring her. She always tried to get as much pleasure as she could in life—from sex, food, travel—while still being responsible. She didn't hold herself back.

This time, they didn't speak much as he trailed kisses along her collarbone, her breasts, and her shoulders. When she started to squirm, he didn't make her wait; his hand was immediately between her legs, and when her lips parted, he smiled at her reaction.

She was very wet for him.

He watched her face as he stroked her. When his thumb circled her clit, she let out a jerky gasp, and that seemed to please him, too.

She hadn't expected the variety in their sexual activities, hadn't anticipated quite how much she'd enjoy being with him. And there was an unfamiliar comfort in being naked with David. Not that she was usually self-conscious, but it wasn't quite as comfortable as this.

Her back bowed off the bed. She was very, very close...

He withdrew.

"Bastard," she muttered.

"Shh." He placed a finger—one that was coated in her moisture—to her lips before reaching for a condom. He rolled it on and slid inside her, touching her clit again as he did so, and she immediately cried out.

"If you were on the other side of the wall," she said, "you would have heard that."

"Yes. But then I wouldn't be inside you."

He kissed her as he thrust in and out, and it wasn't long before he came, pulling her over the edge, too.

"David," she said afterward, when she was lying with her head on his chest. "Can I ask you a personal question?"

"Go ahead," he said.

"When I met you, I thought you were the kind of guy who looked like a husband. Why aren't you married? You have nice hair and you're good in bed." She tried to make her voice light, but when he didn't immediately reply, she said, "You don't have to say anything, if you don't want."

"I'm divorced."

Somehow, that possibility hadn't occurred to her.

"How long ago was that?" she asked.

"Four years. We were together for nine years, married for five. We met in grad school."

They were quiet for a moment.

Had his ex hurt him terribly?

David chuckled. "I know you want to pry. I can see the questions on your face."

"That doesn't mean you need to answer them."

"I know, but..." He ran a hand through his hair. "I'm the one who ended it, when I realized she'd never truly stand up to her family for me. She would always pick them, in the end. She's white, and her parents are racist assholes. I could tell myself it wasn't a big deal when we lived on the other side of the country, but when I got a job in Toronto and we came here, not far from them..." He shook his head. "The worst was the thought of what they'd say to our children."

"I can imagine," Nicole said.

"And because I know you want to ask, no, I don't still love her."

She hadn't considered asking that question, but yes, she'd wanted to know, and she felt relieved. Not because Nicole wanted David to fall in love with her, but because she didn't want him to hurt too much.

"I cut out the racist people in my family," she said.

"You told me."

"Right. When Aunt Eliza got my number. She's one of those Asian ladies who would have only ever married a white man, and she thinks that makes her superior to her cousins, which... Sorry."

He reached out and squeezed her arm.

"It's different with my parents, I think," Nicole said. "My mom just happened to fall in love with a white guy, but she doesn't expect me or Cam to do the same. My aunt is toxic in so many ways. She doesn't approve of my appearance because I'm not dainty and petite, and she thinks I look slutty no matter what I wear, because my breasts are large. Since I'm not super pale, she also thinks I'm too dark, and... Anyway. My mom, for all the issues I had with her, was pretty good at shutting that shit down, but my parents didn't completely stop speaking to Eliza until..." Nicole didn't feel like talking about what had happened with Cam, and David wasn't one to push.

"You're incredibly beautiful," he said.

"Trust me, I fucking know." She thought of how hot she looked in the pin-up painting in her closet. "You don't need to reassure me."

"I know you know, but I want to tell you anyway."

She snuggled up against him. "This is the perfect arrangement. Being friends, living next door to each other, and having sex. It's very convenient."

"Convenient," he repeated faintly. "Yes."

"I love sex, but I don't want everything to be a one-night stand. I used to be fine with that, but then I got old and cranky and tired of flirting. Whenever I found a guy to fuck regularly, he always fell for someone else shortly afterward. Super annoying."

Something occurred to her, and she lifted her head to look at him. "That's cool with you, right? Friends with benefits?"

"Yeah," he said. "Sounds good."

But though he'd agreed with her, she couldn't help feeling slightly disappointed. Perhaps she'd seen too many rom-coms over the years—not that she particularly liked them, but Cam and her mother did—and that part of her had expected him to say that no, he was in love with her, he'd known from the moment she'd handcuffed him to the bed and fed him chocolate mousse.

A ridiculous thought. It wasn't like she wanted that to happen.

As she'd told him, they had the perfect arrangement.

"Have you ever been married?" he asked.

She snorted. "Me? Ha! Marriage would destroy me."

"Why do you say that?"

"I lived with a guy once. We were together for two years. Calvin was your age when we started dating, and I was twenty-two."

"That's a big age difference."

"Yeah, I should have seen it as a warning sign, but I was desperate to be loved." She laughed ruefully. "Especially because my mom and I weren't getting along at the time. I'd moved home for grad school at U of T, but after my mom and I had a big fight, I moved in with Calvin."

Calvin had always talked about how rough it was for Asian men...and he had a point. But really, he just wanted to get away with all the shit that privileged white men could. He hadn't treated her well.

"I felt like that relationship consumed my life," Nicole told David. "Like I lost my identity when I was with him, but I didn't fully realize it until we broke up. Though who am I, anyway? In undergrad, I wasn't the same person as in high school, when I was the nerdy kid who got high marks and didn't have many friends. I certainly didn't kiss anyone back in high school."

Back then, Mom had complained that Nicole wasn't social

enough, that she rarely went out with friends and sometimes ate lunch alone. Mom said Nicole needed to work on her people skills...but high school was a tough time for many people. Not everyone felt like they belonged, and Nicole was made to feel like there was something wrong with her, but there wasn't.

"I was the nerdy kid in high school, too," David said.

She smiled. "I would have expected nothing less."

David, she figured, hadn't gone through the sorts of phases that she had. He'd probably been more constant in who he was.

"You want to hear how I broke up with Calvin?" she asked. "It's a good story."

"Go ahead."

"He decided we should open up our relationship, even though I'd never expressed any interest in that. There was another woman he wanted to fuck, you see. So, it was either we break up or I let him sleep with other people."

"That asshole," David muttered, and she smiled again at his vehemence. It seemed out of character for him, and she couldn't help being thrilled that he was angry on her behalf.

"I reluctantly agreed. I'm sure he never expected me to take advantage of it, but I did. I got some cute outfits, went out, met guys... I wasn't very sexually experienced before Calvin, and when I started fucking other men, I realized just how great sex could be. Anyway, he was all pouty about the action I was getting, and the woman he wanted wouldn't sleep with him. We broke up, and I loved being single. I've been single ever since. It's great having my own space, and I like not answering to anyone. Not having to plan my life around someone else's or worry about his reactions to every little thing."

It was hard to breathe for few seconds because in the past year, Nicole had started to feel lonely. Her life wasn't quite as amazingly awesome as she pretended.

But she did have David now, right next door, and their Friday dinners were nice. She didn't feel as alone now as she had a few months ago.

"Well, I'm glad you dumped him," David said.

"Me, too."

He picked up the framed picture on her night table. It was a photo of her and Cam on holiday last year. "Is this your—"

"Sibling," Nicole said. "Their name is Cam."

"Ah. You look alike. Very much like siblings."

"We do."

"Are they older or younger?" he asked.

"Two years younger."

"Like me and my sister."

"Is your sister in Toronto?"

"No." David set the photo back down. "She's out in Vancouver, where we grew up. She's married, got a couple of kids." There was something wistful in his voice.

"Do you want kids?"

"Yeah, one or two. But I'm already forty, and I don't want to be a super old father. If it doesn't happen in the next five years, well, that's life."

She was about to ask if he'd dated since his divorce. If he was bitter—he didn't seem to be, though.

But then she decided she didn't really want to know.

And it wasn't relevant. It wasn't like he wanted to date *her*, and he seemed to have no problem with their arrangement. That was all that mattered.

He absently stroked her back for a minute, and then her phone vibrated. She pulled it off the bedside table and read the text.

I was really drunk last night, wasn't I? Rose said. *Ahhh, I never get that drunk. Did I make a fool of myself?*

Nicole was about to send a quick reply, but the phone rang in her hands, catching her off guard. She answered.

"Hello?"

"Nicole, I'm soooo sorry," said a familiar voice. Kelsey? "Po Po stole my phone while I was sleeping and wouldn't give it back until I drove her here."

"Buzz us in!" Po Po shouted. "Oh, it's okay, a nice man is holding the door open for me."

The call ended.

"Shit," Nicole said. "Shit, shit. My grandma and cousin are here." She looked down at her naked body and David's, then jumped up and started pulling on clothes. Underwear, bra, yoga pants, sweater. That should be good enough.

"You've got sex hair." David came up behind her and ran his fingers through her hair. "Do you want me to hide in the closet? Attempt make it next door before they arrive?"

She sighed. "I'm not sure if there's time. You might run into them in the hallway, and they've already met you. You can stay, just put on some clothes."

He had to leave the bedroom to find the clothes she'd torn off last night.

"You have mouthwash?" he asked.

"Yep, under the bathroom sink."

"Uh, Nicole?" he said as he stepped into the bathroom. "There's a dildo on the counter."

16

DAVID LAUGHED as Nicole ran into the washroom and grabbed the candy cane dildo to return it to its proper place.

"Oh my God," she said. "That could have been a disaster. Though perhaps my grandmother wouldn't have realized what it was. She just would have asked why I had a Christmas ornament out in March." Nicole started laughing, sounding slightly hysterical.

Now dressed and free of morning breath, David came into the bedroom and rubbed her shoulders.

"Hey, it's okay," he said. "We found it, you put it away. Anything else?"

Just then, there was some vigorous knocking on the front door, and David followed Nicole out of the bedroom.

She opened the door to reveal Po Po and Kelsey.

"Are you surprised?" Po Po asked.

"Yes, very surprised," Nicole said, and David tried not to laugh at her tone.

"Ah, David, you are here, too. Nice to see you again. You are her boyfriend now?"

"No, he's not. We're friends."

"It is just very *suspicious*. I surprise you with visits twice, and both times he is here."

"Indeed," Kelsey said.

Nicole gave her a dark look. "To what do I owe the pleasure of this visit?"

"You are grumpy," Po Po said. "I must have interrupted sex."

This appeared to render Nicole speechless, and David couldn't help feeling amused. After all, this was the woman who'd confidently handcuffed him to her bed last night.

"No, no," he said, since she was incapable of forming words. "I'm just stopping by because we're going to H-Mart. We'll catch an Uber back together to save money." He hoped that sounded believable.

Kelsey twisted her lips, but Po Po said, "Yes, this is smart."

He congratulated himself on the "saving money" part.

"We talked about getting bungeoppang on the way, too," he said, really getting into this domestic fantasy and hoping it would distract Kelsey from any suspicions she had.

"What's bungeoppang?" Kelsey asked.

"It's like taiyaki," he said. "There's a little place on the walk to H-Mart."

"What is taiyaki?" Po Po asked Kelsey. "I've never had it." She pushed her granddaughter's shoulder to get her attention.

"It's a pastry in the shape of a fish with sweet red bean paste."

"That sounds like a good breakfast to me," Nicole said.

He imagined buying her one, hot off the grill, and the orgasmic sounds she'd make as she bit into it.

Kelsey frowned. "Why would you take an Uber back from H-Mart? Isn't it really close?"

"Yeah, it's not too far," he said, "but it's annoying to carry all the bags back."

Po Po stabbed his bicep with her finger. "Wah, are you not strong enough? Nicole, tell him to build bigger muscles!"

He didn't mind her light-hearted teasing. Nicole's family was infinitely preferable to Steph's. Not that he and Nicole were together, but somehow, he'd manage to meet her grandmother. Twice.

"Po Po, stop it," Nicole said.

"You know what we should do? We have a car. We will all go to H-Mart together and drive you home! And you will show me where to get these fish pastries. A fun family trip."

"It's really not—"

"I insist! Why waste money on Uber when you have Kelsey to drive you around?"

"That's me," Kelsey said in a world-weary voice. "The chauffeur."

"Aiyah," Po Po said, "why do you sound so blue? You are living rent free."

"You woke me up at eight in the morning on a Sunday, stole my phone, and demanded I drive you halfway across the city."

"Once we get home, do not worry, I will leave you alone for the rest of the day."

"Sure, Jan." Kelsey rolled her eyes.

"Who is Jan?"

"So, uh," Nicole said, "why *are* you here early on a Sunday morning?"

"It's not early," Po Po protested.

"It's nine thirty. It's early for a Sunday."

"She wanted to bring you bok choy." Kelsey lifted up the plastic bag she was holding. "There was a deal at the store yesterday. And there's a new video she wanted to show you, too."

"Yes!" Po Po said. "Kelsey posted it last night."

"She also wanted to sneak in questions about David or knock on his door, but she told me not to tell you that."

Nicole opened her mouth, but no words came out.

David rather enjoyed seeing her riled up, but he put a calming hand on her shoulder. Though maybe this wasn't the best way to convince Nicole's family that the two of them weren't together.

"But he is already here!" Po Po said. "Am so happy you are still together."

"We're not—"

"Ah, save it, Nicole, I know the truth." Po Po tapped her finger against her temple.

"We're not together," David said. "Now, what is this video?"

Kelsey whipped out her phone and showed them. The video began with Kelsey holding out her hand to display two plastic spiders.

David could see exactly where this was going.

On screen, Kelsey used sticky tack to put one of the spiders on the kitchen wall.

The video then jumped to Po Po hitting the fake spider with a wok.

"You see what I have to put up with?" Po Po said. "She pranked me with fake spider! That's why I woke her up this morning and made her take me here. Now we must all go to H-Mart, and Kelsey, you must buy me *two* of those fishy pastries."

"I can get them for you," David said. They were only a toonie each. And he was happy to go on this unplanned shopping trip. Any time he got to spend with Nicole was nice.

"Ah, good. I knew I liked you." Po Po patted his shoulder.

"No more videos of you drooling over Jason Momoa, Po Po?" Nicole asked.

"Jason Momoa? Ah, right. Hunky actor. Kelsey has not shown me any." Po Po sniffed.

"I saw a guy who looked like him last night, when I was out with my friends."

Oh? This wasn't something she'd told David.

Po Po looked between David and Nicole. "Did you make out with the Jason Momoa guy? He should be on your freebie list!"

David managed to refrain from making a strangled sound.

"You know, like on *Friends*," Po Po continued. "A list of five celebrities you are allowed to have sex with even if you are in a relationship. Wah, I should not have to explain this stuff to you. You should know."

"I didn't kiss him," Nicole said, "But freebie lists aren't relevant anyway. First of all, David isn't my boyfriend, so why would we have these lists? I'm a free woman. I can do whatever I want. Second of all, the freebie list doesn't include look-a-likes. Just the actual celebrities themselves."

"But you have...what do you call it? Plausible deniability?"

"No, I don't think that's quite right..."

"I wish I'd been recording this," Kelsey said.

David couldn't help being glad that Nicole hadn't slept with this Jason Momoa look-a-like but instead had come home to him. He tried not to make too much of it, though.

"I can say it all again and you can record this time," Po Po said. "I have good memory." She tapped her head.

"We tried this once before," Kelsey said, "and it wasn't at all the same. But this has reminded me that I should show you more pictures of actors and record your reaction. People seemed to enjoy that. Now, how about that trip to H-Mart?"

A few minutes later, they all headed down to the visitor parking area.

"Sorry for getting us into this shopping trip," David murmured to Nicole as they followed Kelsey and Po Po to the car.

"Could have been worse," Nicole muttered. "She could have found the dildo."

"What did you say?" Po Po looked back at them. "Are you gossiping about me?"

"Of course not!"

Nicole turned back to David. Last night she'd been incredibly sexy in that red dress, but she was lovely this morning, too, wearing her beret and her winter jacket.

She smiled at him, and he smiled back.

Friends with benefits, he reminded himself.

He could see himself falling for her—he was already falling for her a little—but she'd made it very clear how she felt about relationships, and he wouldn't let himself ruin it.

They had a good thing going on, and he'd simply enjoy what they had.

Sex and bungeoppang and all.

~

"Nicole!" Mom's voice boomed over the phone.

Well, this was exactly what Nicole needed right now. How fun.

She'd been home for all of ten minutes and had just finished putting away her purchases from H-Mart. She'd felt the compulsion to buy lots of food—even though she'd gone grocery shopping a few days ago—because David's mention of taking an Uber made it seem like she was in need of a big shopping trip. She'd been trying to make their story believable, that was all. That was the only reason she'd bought so many frozen dumplings and snacks. Surely these yuzu candies and sweet potato chips that David recommended wouldn't be any good. No way. Just like the shrimp chips. They were terrible.

Ha. She'd already eaten a quarter of the bag.

Nicole plopped down on the couch and set the chips aside.

"Hi, Mom," she said.

The timing of this call was unusual, as Mom typically called on weekday evenings. Most likely, Po Po had called her during the drive home and told her about David.

"When do I get to meet your special friend?" Mom giggled.

Yup, it was just as Nicole had feared.

"I don't know what you're talking about," she said, even though feigning innocence wouldn't get her very far.

"Nicole! You literally just got home from H-Mart with your grandmother and a *boy*."

"David's not a boy. He's forty years old."

"Ooh, I'm starting to get details."

"He lives next door, we hang out sometimes. By sheer coincidence, he happened to meet Po Po again."

"He sounds very nice. Ma is pleased that he bought her fish pastries and pushed her cart."

"He's very nice, yes," Nicole said.

"You deserve someone nice."

There was a long pause, and Nicole thought back to what had happened with Calvin, all those years ago.

When Nicole was in high school, her mother had really gotten into the idea that you could attract good things with positive thinking and visualization.

If it was just that, it would have been fine.

But Mom had also believed that bad things happened to you because of the way you thought, and whenever something bad happened to Nicole, she'd get blamed for it.

You're sick? It's all your fault.

Some guy is being creepy? Must be your fault.

You had to deal with a racist asshole? Must be your fault.

And so Nicole told her mom nothing, but she internalized a lot of the stuff that was said to her.

Calvin, on the other hand, didn't blame her for everything. Just a lot of things, and that felt like an improvement.

After breaking up with Calvin, in a moment of weakness, Nicole told her mom about a lot of what had happened and said she must have deserved it.

She hadn't expected sympathy, but she got it.

Then she and her mom had a big fight, Nicole yelling about how her mother's beliefs had made her feel like shit, how it was basically all victim blaming, how she couldn't help feeling like everything bad about her relationship with Calvin was her own fault, etc.

After that, Mom started to change her views.

Their relationship had improved somewhat since then, but Nicole still hesitated before telling her mom anything, fearing her reaction. And she still sometimes felt like things she had no control over were her own fault.

"Really, you deserve someone nice," Mom repeated.

"I don't want *anyone*, as I've been telling you for the past ten years. Not everyone is meant for a relationship." Nicole angrily stuffed a shrimp chip in her mouth.

"But I'm not sure that's true about *you*. I'm your mother."

"Alright, Mom. I'll keep that in mind."

"You're using your *I'm-just-humoring-you* voice."

"Oh. Am I."

"There it is again!"

This time, Nicole laughed.

"But really," Mom pressed, "not every man is like Calvin. You know that, right?"

"Of course. Not all men."

"One bad relationship doesn't mean all relationships will be the same."

"I know," Nicole said.

"Do you want me to come over? It seems like you could use some company."

"No, because you'd eat my delicious shrimp chips. Besides, I already saw Po Po, Kelsey, and David today. It's time to relax, and you know you're not very relaxing."

"So you've told me."

That was the thing about Mom and Po Po: they were exhausting. If Nicole didn't stand up for herself, they could rearrange her life in seventeen different ways in a single conversation.

"I think I'll have a bath now and watch a movie," she said to her mother. "Talk to you later in the week, okay?"

"Yes. And next time I see you, I have a new moisturizer to give you. Don't let me forget."

It would probably be good stuff, knowing her mom.

Nicole ended the call, then headed to the washroom and started a bath.

The last time she'd had a bath was after she'd first slept with David, and she couldn't help thinking of him now.

She could always count on David to be on her side. He was rather sweet in that regard. And she didn't have to worry about him acting inappropriately or trying to force her to do something she didn't want to do.

The first time she'd seen him in the hall, she'd had no idea they would become friends. Certainly, ending up in bed together was the last thing she'd expected.

She froze in the middle of taking off her clothes.

Roy had ended things because he'd met someone else, and he hadn't been the first man to meet the love of his life while having a no-strings-attached arrangement with Nicole

One day, surely, David would fall in love with someone else, too.

It sounded like he'd be happy to be married again. Have a couple of children. He didn't struggle with commitment.

And he really was a wonderful guy. A catch. If he fell in love with a woman, she'd probably love him back.

Yes, one day David would end their physical relationship, perhaps sooner rather than later, and the thought hurt more than it had with any of her other sex partners.

Nicole told herself it was just because he was right next door and the sex was particularly good, so it was better than any of her other arrangements. Plus, they were friends, but they could continue to be friends.

Surely those were the only reasons that the shrimp chips and bungeoppang were forming a lump in her stomach.

17

IT WAS A COLD, blustery day in March, and when David opened his door for Nicole, she had her arms wrapped around her and looked a touch bedraggled.

Still absolutely lovely, of course.

This was their first Friday dinner since they'd started sleeping together—he'd had that alumni dinner last week—and he couldn't help feeling nervous.

He'd obsessed quite a bit about the food. He'd decided that some kind of soup would be in order, then debated the options for far too long.

"What did you order?" she asked as she took off her boots and coat.

"Pho," he said.

Her face lit up, and David felt like even if he'd spent ten hours figuring out dinner, it would have been worth it. As it was, he'd spent a fair amount of time even once he'd settled on pho. There were countless pho restaurants in Toronto. Finally, he'd decided it would be best if he picked between the two restaurants that were within walking distance of their building—and that decision hadn't been quick, either.

She sat down beside him at the counter. She was still wearing her work clothes. The gray skirt suit looked lovely on her, but he wanted to take it off.

And he didn't chastise himself for having such thoughts now.

He set her bowl in front of her before opening up a container with two fresh spring rolls and dipping sauce, the shrimp and vegetables visible through the rice paper.

"Oh, I haven't had these in ages!" She reached for one, dipped it in a generous amount of sauce, and took a big bite, holding her hand underneath to catch anything that fell.

He loved her delight in the food. Nicole definitely knew how to enjoy herself.

At that thought, his pants felt a bit tight.

"How has your week been?" she asked as he started his pho.

"Not bad. Wednesday was particularly good."

"Was it?" She waggled her eyebrows. "Do tell."

"You know what happened." Wednesday night, she'd sent him a text saying she was horny, and five minutes later, they were in her bed together.

"You're turning pink."

"It's the steam from the pho," he said.

"Sure it is."

It was a little different eating with her now, but there was still an easy companionship between them. What if she came home to him every evening?

He didn't let himself dwell on the possibility.

"Any plans for the weekend?" she asked.

"I have a reference letter to write, and I'll try to actually make it to the pool."

"I'll take that as a challenge."

"I don't have to go quite as early as usual, but lane swimming stops at nine thirty, so it has to be before then."

"Don't worry, you don't have to change your life for me. That's cool. I won't stay the night if you don't want me to."

"I want you to stay," he said quickly. He didn't want there to be any mistake about that.

"Alright. I won't get up too late, and I won't wear you out *too* much." She winked at him, then sighed in pleasure at her first bite of pho. "You always make good food choices."

"I take that as a great compliment."

"As you should."

When they were finished dinner, he cleared everything away and brought out dessert.

"Oh!" she cried. "It looks like art. It's almost too pretty to eat."

"Well, then." He held it away from her. "You don't need to have any."

She gave him a dark look that made him laugh as he set the pastries on a plate.

There were three, because he hadn't been able to decide on only two, from a place that called itself a Eurasian bakery.

"Tell me what everything is," she said.

He pointed at the first one. "This is called the mocha latte." It was made to look like a latte, complete with leaf-like latte art. "The cup is chocolate, and inside there's espresso cream and more chocolate."

She pointed at the second pastry.

"Pandan and coconut," he said.

"The last one looks like strawberry."

"Yep. Strawberry cheesecake."

"That's why there's a mouse for decoration! Because of the cheese."

It was easy to bring a smile to her face, but that didn't mean he liked it any less.

"I assume we're sharing all three?" she said.

"Rather than you eating everything? Yes." He got out two small spoons and passed one to her. His fingers brushed hers, and it felt like a crackling warm fire.

"I would never do that," she said in a silky voice. "Of course I'd let you have at least a bite. Of one of them."

She shifted her stool close to his, and they ate the pastries from the single plate. After she'd tried each of them, he asked, "Which do you like best?"

"The mocha latte one."

"I prefer the strawberry cheesecake."

"So, you're saying I can eat the rest of the other two? Okay." She patted his shoulder.

He did enjoy their affectionate teasing. And sharing cute desserts seemed rather romantic, but he reminded himself that she didn't want romance.

She slid her spoon into her mouth and groaned, then slowly licked the cream from her lips.

"Are you attempting to seduce me, Nicole?" he asked.

"Attempting? I *am* seducing you. I know I'm succeeding." She looked pointedly at his crotch.

"It's true. You are."

He took the spoon from her hands and set it down on the plate. Then he cupped her cheeks and brushed his thumb over her skin.

"You're too effective at your seduction," he murmured. "I won't let you finish eating."

"You're making me give up my chocolate? What the fuck is this?"

He didn't say anything, just removed her suit jacket and started unbuttoning her blouse. He placed her clothes on the empty stool on the other side of her.

"Still too much clothing." He leaned over to kiss her and take off her bra. She tasted of dessert and *Nicole*, and it was a delightful combination. "Now stand up and remove your skirt and underwear."

She did as told, and he came to stand behind her and slid his hand between her legs.

"Now you can eat," he said. "See? You can have sex and chocolate at the same time."

He couldn't see her expression, but she lifted a bite to her lips.

"Mmmmm," she said, drawing it out.

"That's right. Enjoy yourself." He slipped his fingers through her folds and circled her clit with his thumb.

She had a few more bites of dessert, but then she started to tremble in his arms and put the spoon down, which made him feel pretty damn good about his skills.

She arched her neck, and he kissed her along the side of it as he stroked one hand over her breast and thrust two fingers from his other hand inside her.

"David," she said softly.

This orgasm didn't seem as intense as some of her other ones, but he was just getting started.

"You want to finish dessert now?" he asked. "Or can it wait until afterward?"

David kept his voice calm, but fuck, he wanted her to touch him. He wasn't used to being so overcome with need.

He turned her toward him and gave her a little smirk that he thought would piss her off.

Sure enough, she shoved him against the nearest wall and started kissing him, and he smiled against her lips.

At eight o'clock on a Saturday morning, David would normally be heading to the pool, but he'd let himself stay in bed with Nicole just a little longer. They'd had sex, and now she was lying with her chest pressed against his side. He wouldn't have it any other way.

"So, this is your bedroom," she said.

"You've been in here nearly twelve hours."

"But I was distracted by other things." She danced her fingers down his chest. "Is that a rock collection on your dresser?"

"Part of it, yes. I moved the rest of it to the living room, just in case..." He glanced at their shared wall.

She sat up. "Are you saying that my sexcapades made you fear for the safety of your *rock* collection?"

"Well, I was more worried than I ought to have been. It's very, very unlikely anything would have happened, but..."

She let out a big laugh, and he laughed along with her.

"I'm so sorry." She put a hand to her chest and was clearly trying to school her expression into something serious, but she was utterly failing at it.

It was adorable.

"Don't be," he said.

She lay back down. "Why geology? Is that what you always wanted to do?"

"I was always fascinated by the timescale of it. The dinosaurs died out sixty-six million years ago—I learned about that as a kid, though the timing of the extinction has been refined since I first learned of it. And it's hard to truly understand what sixty-six million years means when you've been on Earth for only six years. If the history of the planet were one day long, humans would exist for only a minute or two. Such a tiny, tiny fraction."

"Doesn't it make you feel insignificant?"

"Yeah, but I like that."

"Why?" she asked.

"I don't know. Maybe because it makes one crappy day in my life seem like nothing. And all those millions upon millions of years... It's kind of amazing."

"What kind of research do you do? I might not understand, but try me."

"Geochronology," he said.

"Like, dating rocks?"

"Yeah. Potassium-argon dating is a common method. One of

the isotopes of potassium decays into argon and has a long half-life, so you can look at the relative percentages of potassium and argon in a rock."

"That's cool. I have a science background, so the basics of that make sense."

"But then you got a degree in financial math."

She sighed. "I had this idea that I wanted to do physics research, but after two summers of that—you know, the NSERC program for undergrad students—I decided I just didn't like it enough to do a PhD."

"There are other things you could have done with an engineering physics degree."

She shrugged. "I was good at it, but I had no special love for it. Engineering physics had the reputation of being the hardest engineering discipline at my school, which is partly why I picked it. I wanted to prove I could do it—and kick ass at it."

"Prove to who?"

"Everyone. Including myself, my parents. They—especially my mom—were always like, 'yeah, sure, good grades, honey,' but never focused much on marks. I wanted them to be impressed for once, and I always liked playing with numbers and data. My job is a good fit, and this one allows me a better work-life balance than the last one I had." She paused. "When I was a kid, there were several years when I'd grab the sports section in the paper as soon as I woke up."

"I didn't know you were a sports fan."

"I'm not. I just liked the big tables of sports stats, understanding what they all meant. I enjoyed elections, too. Elections are different now that I'm adult, now that I understand how they affect me, but back then, it was just cool numbers and colored maps."

He wrapped an arm around her and held her close. "I'm enjoying the image of you lying on the carpet, studying MLB stats in the paper with intense concentration."

This led to new fantasies of him and Nicole. Of them reading or working side by side in silence, occasionally looking up to smile at each other.

He tried not to think about that too much.

Like, he was fantasizing about *reading* together?

And then she'd come over, sit on his lap, and say he looked good with his glasses before taking them off.

Ah. That's why he'd been thinking about them reading side by side.

It was really a sex fantasy.

At least, that was what he'd tell himself.

Nicole's phone vibrated, and she grabbed it from beside the bed. "Kelsey sent me a new video of my grandmother. You want to watch?"

"Sure."

On the screen, Po Po was shown a picture of Randall Park in WandaVision.

"He is cute," Po Po said. "Eight out of ten. He looks like the kind of guy you should marry." She looked meaningfully at Kelsey.

Nicole smiled as she set her phone away. "Alright, I should stop distracting you and let you go to the pool."

David missed her presence as she swung her legs over the side of the bed.

But then she said, "Maybe I'll see you tomorrow?"

And he couldn't help but smile.

They were friends with benefits, and he had everything under control…right?

18

NICOLE WALKED down Ossington with a spring in her step. It was still light out, and the weather was warming up. There were crocuses in front of her building now, and she'd seen her first daffodil on the walk to the subway. Yes, April was nice.

Though to be honest, it was partly the regular sex that was putting her in a good mood.

And her grandmother hadn't stopped by unexpectedly when she was naked in bed with David again, so that was a plus.

When she stepped inside the cider bar, she scanned the room and quickly found Sierra. Her friend was sitting at the bar and had already finished more than half her pint.

"You got here early," Nicole said.

"Yeah, figured I'd get a head start on drinking." Sierra had a gulp of cider.

"Something wrong?"

"Oh, the usual. Family dinner last night, and my mom was going on and on about Grace Chau. Grace Chau this, Grace Chau that. She's pregnant again and got a promotion. Or was it her husband who got a promotion? I kinda tuned out."

Grace was the daughter of Sierra's mom's best friend. In her mom's eyes, Sierra—who was divorced, childless, and ran a greeting card shop—had always fallen short of Grace.

"Hey," Nicole said. "You know what? I bet Grace isn't going to have as good of a Saturday night as you are."

Sierra chuckled.

"Do your parents know about Colton?" Nicole asked.

Sierra shook her head.

"Would they be impressed?"

"He's super rich," Sierra said, "and my mom likes money and getting things for free, so yeah. But I'm saving that for when I really need it. I don't like telling my mom when I'm dating some-one. She'd call every day to ask when I'm getting married."

The bartender came over. "Can I get you anything?"

Nicole quickly scanned the tap list. "I'll have the strawberry Earl Grey cider."

Sierra pointed to her glass. "I'll have another one of these. Thank you." When they were alone again, she said, "You want to see the trailer for my movie?" She pulled out her phone and brought up the trailer on YouTube.

Sierra Wu, the fictional character, stood on a hill looking out at the Golden Gate Bridge—Hawk Hill, if Nicole remembered correctly from the trip she'd taken to San Francisco with Cam last year. The sky was gray and evocative. A demon appeared out of nowhere, and Sierra Wu slayed it with a quick movement of her sword.

"Maybe if I saved humanity from demons," Sierra muttered, drinking more cider, "then I'd be good enough for my mother."

"Hey!" It was Amy, and she'd brought her husband with her today. "Ooh, it's the trailer. I've already watched it like seventeen times."

On screen, a scowling East Asian man with golden skin appeared. He wasn't wearing a shirt. This, Nicole presumed, was Rebel, Sierra Wu's love interest.

"You're hotter," Amy murmured to Victor.

"I know. You've told me way more than seventeen times." He kissed the top of her head.

The movie trailer didn't give away the plot. Rather, it had lots of tense music and special effects and made everything seem very exciting without giving you any idea of what was happening, unless you had read the books.

Five minutes later, after Rose, Charlotte, and Mike had arrived, they were shown to a table. Nicole was about to sit down when a man approached her. A dark-haired, blue-eyed white guy who looked like he moved easily through the world and was probably at least a little cocky.

"Hey, there," he said. "Can I buy you a drink?"

Nicole did look pretty fabulous today. She was wearing jeans that made her ass look great, plus a sleeveless black shirt and a colorful scarf, and she was having an excellent hair day.

She tossed her hair over her shoulder. "Sorry, I'm not interested."

He looked like he was about to protest and try to make his case, but when she ignored him, he walked away.

She breathed out a sigh of relief, then noticed all her friends were staring at her.

"What?" Nicole said. "I can turn a guy down."

"Of course," Rose said, "but he's not the sort of guy you'd usually turn down."

"Besides," Sierra added, "you didn't even take a second look at that bartender earlier, and he's just your type, beard and all."

"It's because of that man." Charlotte snapped her fingers. "David, right? The one you told me about back in January, who brought you an ube birthday cake and met your grandmother."

Now every head swiveled toward Charlotte.

"Excuse me?" Sierra said. "You've been sitting on this information for three months?"

"Well, it was more like two and a half."

"Charlotte!"

"What? Nicole made me swear not to tell. And it was her birthday, and she was helping me buy clothes, so I kept my promise."

"Until now." Nicole had a generous sip of cider.

Rose put a finger to her chin. "You know, I haven't seen you make a move on a guy in over a month."

The man whom Nicole had slept with before she and David hooked up.

Nicole shrugged. "Whatever. A month or two isn't that long."

"It's a little long for you," Rose said. "I suspect you're getting some and not telling us."

"Tinder is a thing."

"No, I think it's this David guy, and the fact that you wouldn't let Charlotte tell us is definitely fishy."

"I knew your romantic brains would take it the wrong way, just because a guy brought me a cake and accidentally met my grandmother. We're friends."

"Mm-hmm," Sierra said.

"Who are sleeping together, yes. He lives next door, so it's convenient. We share a meal once a week because, like I said, we're friends." Might as well get everything straight now. "Since I'm having good sex on a regular basis, I don't feel the need to seek out other guys. Five years ago, I might have done both, but now it seems like too much hassle."

And, frankly, she wasn't interested.

"So, it's just sex," Amy said. "Plus friendship."

"Yes, that's what I'm telling you."

There were lots of skeptical faces around the table, and Nicole realized just how many of her friends were in relationships. Amy was married. Sierra had a boyfriend. Charlotte—who'd sworn off dating for five years—now had a boyfriend, too. Rose didn't, but she'd always dreamed of romance.

All of a sudden, Nicole felt achingly lonely. Almost like she didn't belong in this group anymore.

But her friends had been great, ever since she'd met them in university, and they'd never judged her for enjoying sex with lots of different men.

She used to have more friends whom she'd seen regularly. Friends from grad school and work. One friend she'd met at a bar back in the day. But they'd moved away, or their lives had changed and they didn't see Nicole as often anymore.

These were the main friends she had left, and she was starting to feel like she'd lose them, too, like they didn't understand her and their lives were going in different places from hers.

And what about David? He was her friend as well, and one day, he'd likely find another woman, maybe get married again.

She ached whenever she thought of it.

She'd been in a good mood when she'd arrived, but now...

"Dinner and sex," Sierra said. "Sounds awful date-like."

"We alternate being responsible for dinner," Nicole explained, "and he always buys something different for dessert. Ube cake, Portuguese egg tarts, mocha latte pastries."

"Mocha latte pastries? Why haven't I heard of these before?" Charlotte demanded.

"He sounds very attentive," Amy said. "Do you have a picture of him on your phone?"

Nicole brought up his page on the Department of Earth Sciences website.

"Oh."

What was that "oh" supposed to mean? When Nicole had first seen David, she hadn't done a double take or anything like that, but now she felt protective of him. Everyone should be impressed with how handsome he was, dammit, even if he wasn't wearing glasses in this picture.

"He doesn't seem like your type," Charlotte said, "but he's good-looking, yes."

"He looks so...wholesome," Amy said, "and he's a professor?"

"David's not wholesome," Nicole protested. "Not in bed, anyway." She felt her cheeks starting to heat, which annoyed her.

"He's different from the men you usually sleep with," Sierra said. "I think that means something. And you're not even looking at other guys. That's not like you. Come to think of it, the night we were at L, you didn't stay as long as usual."

"You weren't flirting with the guy who looked like Jason Momoa," Charlotte put in, "and blamed it on your grandmother's TikTok video. Plus, you were texting David in the washroom."

Amy nodded sagely. "Yeah, you have a crush on him."

It was good-natured teasing. Nicole had ribbed Charlotte about Mike the same way. But she couldn't help clenching her hands under the table. Then she reached for her pint and had a long swallow of sweet cider.

"No, I don't," she said at last.

"It sure took you a while to say that," Sierra mused.

"Stop bugging me about him!" Nicole snapped.

The table was very, very quiet for a moment.

"Does anyone want to order food?" Mike asked, his arm around Charlotte.

"I know relationships aren't your thing," Sierra said to Nicole, "but maybe—"

"Stop it! Why are you so positive about relationships anyway? Your boyfriend was supposed to meet us that night at L, and he was talking to other people practically the whole evening."

"He had important things to do."

"Since he's so rich and important, why doesn't he solve child poverty?"

Rose touched Nicole's shoulder. "We get it. We won't tease you about David anymore."

That was exactly what she wanted, but Nicole felt she was being treated like a child. She petulantly downed the rest of her cider.

She wasn't herself tonight. Her voice sounded flat, and she was drinking faster than usual. She rarely had more than three drinks when she was out, but tonight, she felt lonely in a crowd.

She was gonna get drunk.

The doorbell in Murray's house rang.

"David, could you get that?" Murray asked.

Huh. David had thought it was just supposed to be him, Murray, and Murray's wife, Mildred, for dinner.

He walked to the front door and opened it up.

"Hi!" said the white woman standing on the doorstep. She looked to be in her thirties. "You must be David. I'm Cassie."

David immediately understood why Cassie had been invited and why he'd been asked to answer the door. He smiled politely at her and ushered her inside, but he couldn't muster any enthusiasm.

No, instead he wondered how Nicole's night with her friends was going. What she was wearing. Whether she was enjoying the warm weather.

He took Cassie's coat and led her to the living room. Mildred offered Cassie a glass of wine then made herself scarce; Murray announced that he'd fire up the barbecue and leave the young people alone.

David and Cassie sat on the couch, him with his coffee and her with her wine, and had a pleasant enough conversation. She was a cheerful woman with a big smile, and she worked in a biotech lab with Mildred.

If he'd met her a few months ago, would he have been interested in her?

Possibly.

But now she didn't do anything for him, even though, objectively, she was good-looking. He wished he were trapped in an elevator with Nicole instead, and frankly, who *wished* they were trapped in an elevator?

When Cassie left the room to get more wine, David slipped out the back door and found Murray grilling chicken on the barbecue.

"What do you think?" Murray asked with a wink. "You told me back in the fall that you wanted to date again, but I haven't heard a peep about you going on dates. Those app things aren't working for you, I guess."

"She's nice," David said. "I like her, but not like that."

"Oh. Too bad." Murray opened his mouth, and David figured Murray wanted to ask why, but in the end, he kept silent.

Dinner was pleasant enough, but David found himself focusing on the way Murray and Mildred lightly teased each other, their casual touches. They'd been married for thirty-five years, and he couldn't help thinking about how he wanted that one day.

In fact, as the evening went on, the yearning in his chest increased.

He walked Cassie to the subway at the end of the night.

"I'm, uh, going north," he said as they stepped inside the station.

"I'm going south."

There was a moment of awkward silence.

"It was nice to meet you," he said.

"Likewise."

They left each other with a nod and a smile.

He'd had the sense that Cassie was interested but could tell he didn't feel the same way, and so she didn't press it.

He hoped she found someone.

As he walked down the hallway to his unit, he wondered if Nicole was still out with her friends. It was eleven, so she probably was, but when he passed her door, he doubled back. Might as well knock, just in case.

She opened the door almost immediately, bottle of rum in hand, and stumbled against the doorframe. "David!"

19

DAVID HAD SEEN Nicole drink a glass or two of wine. He'd seen her a little tipsy, but nothing like this, and he was immediately full of concern.

"I'm drunk," she slurred.

"I can see that," he said.

Usually when she answered her door, she looked put together —even if she was wearing yoga pants and a T-shirt—and now that they were sleeping together, she'd often shoot him a saucy smile or wink.

Tonight was a different story.

She was still wearing the shirt he assumed she'd worn out, but she'd put on frayed pajama pants. Her hair was wild, and her make-up was smudged under her eyes.

"You look nice." She poked his chest.

He gently took the rum bottle out of her hand and set it on the counter. He grabbed a glass of water before leading her to the couch.

"You took my rum," she pouted.

"I don't think you need any more tonight. How much did you drink?"

She hiccupped. "I had four ciders at the bar, then I came home and…" She shrugged and pointed at the bottle on the counter before pointing at the empty bag of sweet potato chips on the coffee table. "You're evil. You introduced me to those chips! Now I've eaten three bags."

"You've eaten three bags today?"

"No. You're being silly. In the past month."

He put his arm around her. "Did something happen? Why are you drinking so much?"

"I'm lonely." She didn't poke him in the chest again, but he felt it all the same.

"Well, I'm here now."

She leaned over and tried to kiss him, but he wasn't going to make out with her when she was in this state.

"Drink some water," he said, handing the glass to her.

"You're looking after me," she mumbled.

"Yes, of course I'm looking after you. I'm your friend."

"I saw my other friends tonight. They teased me about you." She scrunched up her nose.

Was she drunk because she was appalled at the thought of being with him, or because she secretly wanted to be with him and that bothered her?

"Did they?" he murmured, rather hoping she'd tell him more.

"But I don't want a relationship." She slapped a fist against the back of the couch. "Most of my friends are in relationships now. They're leaving me."

"I'm sure they're not leaving you."

"I feel lonely, even when I'm with them." She lifted her hand to her mouth, then frowned when she noticed she had a glass of water in her hand. She'd probably been hoping for the rum bottle. "Can I tell you a secret?"

"Of course."

She leaned in and cupped her free hand around his ear, but

she spoke even louder than before. "When I come home to an empty apartment, sometimes it makes me want to cry."

He didn't know what to say, so he stroked her hair. She arched toward him like a puppy enjoying a good scratch.

"You're going to leave me, too," Nicole said with another hiccup.

"No. I'll always be your…friend."

"You're going to leave me," she insisted. "Like Roy. You'll find some other woman." A tear streaked down her face, and he lifted a tissue to wipe it away. "Nobody loves me. Why does no one love me?"

"Your family loves you." They might drive her crazy, but he was sure they loved her. "Your friends love you."

"That's not what I mean. Nobody falls in love with me. They fall in love with someone else, and then they leave me."

It was on the tip of his tongue.

I fell in love with you.

He was startled by how much he wanted to say those words.

But they weren't true, were they? It was just his impulse to make her feel better.

"Someone will love you," he said instead, but he was a little confused. He'd thought she didn't want romantic love.

As if she could read his mind, she said, "I don't want a relationship. Just want to break someone's heart."

A chill went through him. "Why would you want to do that?"

"To know someone could love me." More tears came to her eyes. "I'm terrible."

He pulled Nicole into his lap, and she wrapped her arms around him.

"Do you drink like this often?" he asked.

"Not in…" She burped. "Years."

To be honest, he was glad that she was letting him stay. That she trusted him and allowed him to comfort her. He wasn't used to seeing her vulnerable like this—usually, she was bold and self-assured.

"Drink some more water, then let's get you to bed," he said.

She crossed her arms over her chest. "You can't tell me what to do."

"Sometimes you like it when I tell you what to do."

"Are we having sex tonight?" She put her hands on the hem of her shirt.

He stilled her. "No."

"Because I'm drunk."

"Yes. You're drunk."

"But will you stay over? It will be a..." She squinted as she searched for the word. "Platonic sleepover."

"I can do that."

This seemed to perk her up. She drank more water then headed to the washroom, where he heard her brushing her teeth. That was a good start.

When she emerged ten minutes later, she'd removed most of her make-up, but there was still a small black smudge at the corner of her left eye.

He now had a toothbrush at her apartment because he stayed at least once a week, so he washed up, flossed, and brushed his teeth before entering the bedroom. Nicole had put on a loose shirt with a cartoon alpaca.

"You need a shirt, too," she said. "No naked sleeping tonight." She pulled two shirts out of her drawer. One was a San Francisco shirt with an image of the Golden Gate Bridge; the other was a unicorn shirt.

He took the latter because he thought she'd giggle.

She did. "You're cute." She poked him in the stomach.

"You're very pokey when you're drunk. Anyone ever tell you that?"

She was still giggling. She seemed less morose than she had earlier, so that was nice.

He only wanted her to be happy.

When he lay down in bed and pulled the covers up, she flopped against his side and slung her arm over his chest.

Two minutes later, she was snoring.

～

When Nicole cracked open an eye, sunlight was streaming through her blinds, brighter than usual. She looked at the clock. It was a little after nine.

Well, that wasn't too bad.

She slowly sat up as the events of last night came back to her.

"Oh dear God," she muttered.

She'd gotten drunk. She'd had rum straight from the bottle.

Now she had a slight hangover. She'd certainly had worse back in the day, but she hadn't had a hangover in years. And David…

That was the worst part. Definitely worse than the hangover.

David had come over when she'd had a bottle of rum in her hand. David, who didn't even drink. She'd whined to him about how she was lonely and how no one loved her and how he would leave her.

She'd been such a mess. Pathetic.

Who was this person she'd become? Nicole didn't like her.

No, she was a kick-ass single woman who could take care of herself and enjoyed the freedom of living alone.

David had stayed over, but when she turned to his side of the bed, there was only a folded pink unicorn shirt. He'd probably gone swimming.

Then she noticed the note on the pillow.

Will be back with breakfast soon, it said. *There's Advil and water on the bedside table.*

Why did that note make her so giddy?

Probably because he was going to bring her something delicious, and she was all about good food.

She took the Advil and drank half the water and waited for him to return.

When she heard a key in the lock—he must have taken her keys—her heart kicked up a notch. She considered going out to the kitchen to meet him, then decided they could have breakfast in bed.

"Hey. You're awake." He stood at the doorway to her bedroom, a takeout bag in his hand. "How are you feeling?"

"Not too bad. Just embarrassed. I promise, I don't do that often. What's for breakfast?"

"Pulled pork sandwiches."

"From that new place on Cummer?" Her thirty-four-year-old brain was always amused by that street name.

"Yes."

"Gimme." She held out her hands. She'd read about this restaurant and had been eager to try it.

"Uh-uh. No way am I letting you eat this in bed."

"Fine, fine. Be no fun."

She put on a clean shirt—no bra—then headed to the kitchen. David had already poured her a glass of orange juice and set out her sandwich. He was now making coffee, and she was suddenly struck with the strange thought that he looked like he belonged here.

She shook her head to clear it of that notion, but she couldn't completely make it disappear. He fit into her life so easily, and he seemed to know what she needed without her even saying anything. For example, he'd brought her this amazing pork sandwich.

Well, perhaps she should wait until she'd tried it.

She took a big bite and groaned at the melt-in-her-mouth meaty goodness and crusty bread. Yeah, that was incredible.

"Are there caramelized onions in here?" She licked the sauce off her hand, plus the sauce that was running down her arm. Apparently, she had no shame around David.

"Yes. I read on a food blog that their sandwich is better with caramelized onions, and I know you like onions, so I got the extra topping."

She nodded. "Good call."

"I got the other sandwich without, just in case." He started unwrapping it.

"But you like onions, too, don't you?"

"I think I can manage, Nicole."

"I'm sorry about yesterday. You didn't need to take care of me. I would have been fine."

"I know. You were drunk, but you weren't in danger of throwing up."

"Yet you stayed, even though I was no fun."

"I wanted to stay," he said quietly.

There was something about that—the way he said it, more than the words themselves—that made her uncomfortable. She stopped chewing her delicious sandwich.

"If you ever get drunk," she said with a laugh, trying to lighten the mood, "I owe you."

"I'll keep that in mind."

"You could have gone swimming this morning. You didn't have to buy me breakfast and eat it with me."

He got up to pour their coffee. "You think I'm not enjoying my sandwich?"

"You don't have caramelized onions, so you can't be enjoying it as much as me."

"Well, then." He pulled her sandwich out of her hands and had a bite. "I'm keeping this." But he smiled at her when she grabbed it back.

Why was he so sweet?

Surely he would find a woman to marry, and they'd have those children he wanted.

She nearly shuddered as the things she'd said last night flooded back into her mind.

"How was your dinner with your friend yesterday?" she asked.

"It was good, but he…" David trailed off.

"What?"

"Never mind. It was a good night."

Nicole had finished her sandwich, but a little piece of pork had escaped. She picked it up and licked her fingers afterward, making a show of doing it slowly and sliding her tongue over her upper lip afterward.

David's gaze, predictably, followed her tongue.

Then, to her surprise, he abruptly stood up and drained the rest of his coffee.

"I should go." He jerked his thumb in the direction of his apartment. "I've got some data to review and…um."

She tried to hide her disappointment. "What about tonight? You want to come over after dinner? I promise to be sober this time."

"Okay. Yes. That would be good." He kissed her forehead before heading out the door.

Had she said something wrong? He wasn't usually abrupt like that.

Nah, he was just busy, that was all.

David did have work to do, but instead, he paced his living room.

He feared he was losing control of the situation.

At breakfast, Nicole had been upbeat, despite what had happened last night. As he watched her enjoy her food, he'd almost said something idiotic. Something about these feelings he was starting to have for her.

Last night had changed something. Maybe it was the fact that she'd allowed him to see her in a messy state, to look after her.

Or that he'd woken up next to her even though they hadn't had sex.

Or that she'd told him how she wished someone would fall in love with her.

But at the same time, she was very clear that she didn't want a relationship; she wanted to keep her independence.

If he did fall in love with her, she'd break his heart.

So, no. He would not allow those feelings to take root and grow into more. If he confessed any feelings, she'd probably shut him out, and he didn't want to stop seeing her. Sleeping with her.

You're already too far gone.

No, that couldn't be true.

He was determined to control his feelings. He *had* to.

20

"Hey, can you buzz us in?"

It was Nicole's mother, and unlike certain other visits from her family, this one wasn't a surprise, and Nicole wasn't in bed with a man.

Nope, it was a Sunday afternoon, and she was completely prepared for this visit: she was fully dressed and had done a little light cleaning in her apartment. Her mom had called yesterday to say that she and Dad would bring almond cookies over for tea today.

There was a knock at her door, and Nicole let in her parents...and Cam?

"I didn't know you were coming." Nicole had seen her sibling for lunch yesterday. Cam had told her that they wanted to go on holidays with their partner this year and asked if that was okay, since Cam and Nicole usually traveled together. Nicole had assured them it was fine, despite her disappointment; she and Cam had previously discussed going to Spain this fall.

"Well, I didn't want to miss this," Cam said. "I apologize in advance. I did put up a slight protest, but when they were determined to go ahead with it, I decided to come."

Mom handed Nicole a couple of bags of food and gave her a hug. Curiously, though, Mom didn't take off her shoes. Nope, she put her hand back on the door handle.

"Start the water for tea," Mom said.

"Where are you going?"

"Oh, just to ask your boyfriend next door to join us."

Nicole grasped her mom's arm. "Mom! He isn't my boyfriend."

"I'm aware you think that, dear," Mom said. "But I can still invite him even if he's not technically your boyfriend. His name's David, right? He's met your grandmother twice and he hasn't met me. Doesn't seem fair. I'm the one who gave birth to you. The one you vomited on when you had the stomach flu when you were eight."

"Can you stop holding that against me?" Nicole muttered.

"I need to make sure your *special friend* is good enough for you."

"Oh, no, not this 'special friend' business again."

"You said he isn't your boyfriend. What am I supposed to call him?"

Unfortunately, during this conversation, Nicole had eased up her grip on her mother's arm, and Mom escaped into the hallway.

"Mom!" Nicole shouted.

But Mom was already at the door next to hers.

The wrong door, not David's.

Not wanting to disturb Mrs. Kim, Nicole said, sulkily, "Wrong, way."

Mom hurried to David's door and knocked. Nicole crossed her fingers, hoping David wouldn't be home, but from what she knew of his schedule, he likely would be.

Sure enough, he was.

"Hi, I'm Tammy Louie." Mom stuck out her hand. "Nicole's mother. I was just wondering, since you're Nicole's *special friend*, whether you'd like to join us for tea today?"

Oh, God. Mom had actually done it. She'd said "special friend" in front of David.

Nicole covered her face with her hands. Behind her, Dad and Cam laughed.

"You're supposed to be on my side," Nicole muttered to Cam.

"Sorry," Cam said. "I've gotten so tired of being teased about Tessa that it's nice to see her attention on someone else for a change."

Nicole turned to her father. Throughout her childhood, she'd felt like he was the one who understood her better. The one who explained all those numbers in the sports section to her.

"I wasn't going to stop this," Dad said. "If you're going to date again, I have to make sure he treats you right, unlike the last one." He made a show of cracking his knuckles, which Nicole knew was just for show, but still.

She looked down the hall. David was approaching. She found herself smiling at him, but then she pushed that smile aside.

She'd seen David yesterday. She didn't need to see him again today...with her family.

Well, too late now.

~

David had hesitated when Tammy had shown up at his door and asked him to come over. This was clearly not Nicole's idea. Besides, he found meet-the-parents situations slightly terrifying.

Okay, more than slightly terrifying.

He hadn't even realized until now, but his heart was beating at a disturbing rate.

This was easily explained: when he'd met Steph's parents, it hadn't gone well, and the issues with her parents had ultimately been a major reason their marriage had ended.

He exhaled and reminded himself that Nicole wasn't his girlfriend. However, that thought didn't exactly make him feel good.

And *that* reaction made him feel even worse.

He was supposed to control his feelings for her!

Perhaps he wasn't in the best state of mind for this social event.

"You must be Cam," he said to the person he'd seen in Nicole's photograph. "Nice to meet you." They were wearing jeans, a short-sleeve buttoned shirt, hoop earrings, and glasses with thick frames. They had short brown hair—the same color as Nicole's—that was longer on top.

They shook his hand.

Next, Nicole's father, Scott.

Scott's handshake was extra firm and maybe a little threatening?

Or possibly David was reading too much into the handshake.

Nicole made some tea, and they sat down at her little dining room table. He and Nicole usually ate in the kitchen; he'd never sat here before. He helped himself to a cookie and tried to remain calm, even if he was as anxious as the first time he'd taught a class.

"I hear you're a professor," Cam said. "Which subject?"

They talked about his job for a bit, as well as Cam's—they were an architect—and he started to feel less jittery.

"If you've got tenure," Scott said, "I suspect you're a little older than Nicole."

"Yes, I'm forty."

"You don't look it," Tammy said, "but at least you don't look way younger than your age. I could pass for a teenager until my late thirties, and it was awkward."

"People gave us dirty looks," Scott said, "even though I'm only a year older than her."

"But why *are* you single at forty?" Tammy asked.

"Mom!" Nicole and Cam said in unison.

"I just want to know if there's something wrong with him.

Calvin was the same age, and as we learned, there was a reason he was dating a twenty-two-year-old."

"But I'm not twenty-two anymore. And we're not dating." Nicole sounded exasperated.

"I'm divorced," David said.

Maybe it would have been easier to lie, but lies could come back to bite you later. Sure, he might not see Nicole's parents again, but what if...

Nicole's family members all looked at each other, and Nicole put her head in her hands.

"Why are you divorced?" Tammy asked.

"It's none of your business," Nicole said, angrily grabbing a cookie. "He's told me a little about it, but he doesn't owe you details."

"Hmm," Scott said. "He really must be a *special* friend if he's told you." He and Tammy shared a meaningful look.

David noticed that many of Nicole's features were in between those of her parents. She had her mother's skin tone and eye color, but the shape of her eyes, her nose...those were a combination.

"David?"

Oh, shit. Someone must have asked him a question.

"Sorry," he said. "Could you repeat that?"

"I think he got lost in her eyes," Tammy said, then gave him a gentle shove.

"Mom," Nicole said. "Don't harass my so-called special friend!"

They were all laughing, except Nicole. She looked like she was on the verge of laughter but was trying to control herself.

"We should get going." Tammy patted Nicole's shoulder. "I'm sure you and David have better things to do than entertain us."

"Mom! Stop it!"

This may not be how David had intended to spend the afternoon, but he hadn't minded. Even though it had been a little uncomfortable, it was certainly an improvement over the last time he'd met a woman's parents.

～

"Oh my God." Nicole wanted to tear out her hair. "I'm so sorry you were subjected to that. You could have made up an excuse and declined." She would have defended him if he hadn't wanted to meet her parents.

He sat beside her on the couch. "It's fine. Truly."

"You can go now. I'm sure you're busy." She wouldn't let on that she didn't want him to leave. No, she would not.

"There are more fun things to do than mark exams."

He pulled her into his lap; she hadn't been expecting it, and she let out a giggle, which turned to a moan as he started kissing his way down her neck.

She arched into him. "Make me forget about what just happened."

"I'll do my best."

He pulled her shirt over her head and tossed it on the couch, followed by her bra. Then he lavished attention on her nipples. He sucked one into his mouth and rolled his tongue over the peak, just the way she liked it.

But…

"I need it rough today," she said as she tore off his shirt.

"That can be arranged."

David turned her so she was facing away from him and helped her remove her yoga pants and underwear. He covered her breast with one hand, and the other slid between her legs. She could hear the sound of her moisture as he fucked her hard with his fingers. The sight of his fingers inside her was unbearably erotic, and she made an unintelligible sound as he started kissing her neck and overwhelming her with all he could make her feel.

"Nicole," he murmured. "Ride my hand."

She did as he commanded, and when he touched his thumb to her clit, she jerked in surprise and shuddered as she came.

"I love watching you come," he whispered. "Now, let's go to the bedroom."

As soon as they were in her bedroom, she undressed him. Then she lay back in bed, her legs spread, and he crawled on top of her. And before he kissed her, he looked at her like...

To be honest, she didn't want to think about it too much.

Instead, she shut her eyes as they kissed, and somehow, his kisses seemed deeper than before. Deeper than they did with anyone else, even though that didn't make sense.

She squirmed impatiently, and he chuckled before he returned to kissing her.

She reached for his cock, thick and heavy between his legs. He hissed out a breath when she touched him, as well as when she flicked her other hand over his nipple; she knew his body better now, and she could anticipate how he'd react.

For the past several years, she'd rarely slept with a man more than half a dozen times, but David was different. She'd been in bed with him many times now, and the familiarity was nice.

But that didn't mean the sex was any less exciting. Unlike with Calvin.

Why was she comparing David to Calvin? It wasn't like David was her boyfriend.

She needed these thoughts out of her mind, and as if knowing that, David's hand was between her legs again, while his other hand fumbled with the drawer of her night table. He tossed a bunch of toys on the bed.

When his hand left her body, it was to pick up the largest of the dildos. He took his time coating it with lube, and she couldn't help writhing on the bed as she waited.

"God, I love how much you want it," he said.

And she loved when he talked to her like this.

He ran the toy over her slit before pushing it inside. Her body accepted it easily.

"Yes, that's pretty," he breathed as he maneuvered it inside her.

He swirled his tongue over her clit, and it didn't take long before she was coming again for him.

He left her sensitive clit alone as he slid up her body to kiss her lips, but he kept the toy inside her. Kept her full. She stroked his cock as he kissed her, desperately needing to touch him.

Then he slid down to kiss her pussy again, and with his talented tongue, he brought her to yet another orgasm before crawling back up her body.

He repeated this two more times, and she was practically a quivering mess.

"I want to suck you," she said.

"In a moment. But first…" He held up her anal plug and raised his eyebrows.

She nodded, and he drizzled lube on the toy and worked it into her ass.

"You okay?" he asked.

"Yeah."

"I'm going to fuck your mouth now, alright?"

He didn't swear outside of the bedroom, and that made it all the better when she heard those words fall from his lips, still in the politest of ways, always checking in with her.

He held his cock to her lips. She opened for him, and he put one hand on the back of her head and fucked her mouth, as promised.

As she shifted on the bed, the toys moved inside her and she groaned around his cock. The different sensations were driving her wild. She'd already come five times, but it wasn't enough. Nowhere near enough.

He pulled out of her mouth and started thrusting the dildo inside her again.

"I'd like you to wear the anal plug while I'm inside you," he said. "What do you think? Would you want that?"

As soon as she nodded, he pulled the dildo out of her pussy. It glistened with her moisture. He slid it between her lips and left it there as he rolled on a condom. She bent her legs and lifted them as he sank inside her.

God, that was good.

He pulled the dick out of her mouth and set it aside.

"Does it feel different for you?" he asked.

Or something like that. She couldn't fully process words right now, because it felt so overwhelming. She'd never done it quite like this before, and God, she liked being stretched.

And then she saw him pick up a vibrator.

This was it. She was going to die.

He turned it on at the lowest speed and pressed it to her clit. She came immediately. She hardly knew what was going on anymore.

He let her recover for a minute before he turned it on once more.

"No. It's too much. I can't take it," she sobbed.

"You sure?"

"Yeah."

He didn't use the vibrator again, but he continued to fuck her with gusto, and she was a trembling mess. When he picked up his pace and came inside her, she cried out but didn't come—at least she didn't think she did, but she hardly knew what way was up.

Afterward, he eased the anal plug out of her. "I'll wash the toys."

She collapsed on top of the blankets and tried to recover.

He joined her a little while later.

"You good?" he asked.

"Mmm. Don't make me talk."

He didn't say anything for a few minutes, just wrapped his

naked body around hers and held her close. With the fluffy pillow and the soft blankets… She could lie here forever.

"I love how you're not shy about sex at all," he said. "It's hot."

She flicked her gaze toward the closet and thought about the painting she'd hidden there. The one no one else had ever seen.

But instead of mentioning it, she murmured, "Yeah, I'm a good time."

As she spoke those words, her boneless feeling started to fade.

She was the kind of woman whom men enjoyed in bed, but they didn't fall in love with her. Didn't imagine settling down with her. Despite her outward confidence, that had started to bother her more in the past few months.

Now she was beginning to wish David would fall in love with her, and the scary thing was that she definitely didn't want to break his heart. She couldn't bear the thought of hurting him, and she was bothered by her strong feelings.

Yet, as she lay here with David and he pressed kisses to her neck, it was such a perfect moment that she was—mostly—able to enjoy it for what it was.

She'd save the worrying for another day.

21

THAT WEDNESDAY, David was loading up his dishwasher when there was a knock on the door. He smiled. It was likely Nicole, and she'd drag him to the bedroom. Usually, her visits were planned, though on occasion she stopped by unexpectedly.

But when he opened the door, it wasn't Nicole who greeted him.

It was her grandmother and cousin.

"Did something happen to Nicole?" The words rushed out of him.

"No, she is fine," Po Po said. "Far as I know. But I came to see you. This is a secret from her, okay?"

"I'm really sorry about this," Kelsey said, wringing her hands.

"First of all." Po Po jabbed a finger in his chest then stepped inside. Kelsey helped her take off her shoes. "You and Nicole are not dating?"

"That's correct."

"You cannot fool me. I am eighty-six years old. Lots of life experience. Very smart."

"Yeah, sure," Kelsey said. "That's why you—"

"Silence!" Po Po held up a hand. "I am very smart, and that's why I know that you"—she pointed at David—"have feelings for Nicole."

David was alarmed. What had Nicole's grandmother noticed? Had she seen him looking at Nicole like he wanted to get her naked?

"No." The word felt thick and wrong in his throat, but he had to say it. Because who knew what Po Po would say to Nicole.

"You are lying!" She tried to get up in his face, but this didn't work very well, seeing as she was a foot shorter than him.

"Po Po," Kelsey said, "this isn't the reason you gave me for wanting to see David. You tricked me! Let's leave his feelings alone."

"Ah, so you can see it, too," Po Po said.

"Yes, but clearly he doesn't want to talk about it."

"That's why I must make him. I want another wedding in the family. David, you must tell me the truth, then you must tell Nicole."

He didn't say anything.

"Come on!" Po Po shouted, and now he was worried Nicole might hear, given the thin walls. "Do not make me sad! Have you seen my videos? I post so many videos about how to win arguments—"

"Two," Kelsey interrupted. "There have been two."

Po Po waved this off. "I shall prevail!"

Kelsey started laughing.

"If you don't admit your feelings," Po Po said, "maybe I will have medical emergency. Will it be fake? You don't know. Then you will feel bad. Come on, tell me!"

"Okay, okay," David said, holding up his hands. "Yes, I like Nicole romantically."

"I'm not sure that was an honest confession," Kelsey said. "You basically forced him into it, Po Po. Maybe he just said it to shut you up."

"Wah, what are you saying?" Po Po asked.

David hadn't wanted to admit his feelings to Nicole's grandmother when he already struggled to admit them to himself. Since Nicole had made it clear she didn't want a relationship, he'd been trying to pretend he didn't want more.

But lately, that had become close to impossible. And he hated the fact that Po Po and Kelsey would think he'd lied about his feelings under coercion from an elderly woman.

"I'm being honest," he said. "I have romantic feelings for her, but I don't think she feels the same way. She's had some bad experiences in the past, and I understand."

"Ah, she is a silly girl," Po Po said, "but the next part of my plan will help you win her over."

Hope sprang in his chest, and he immediately tamped it down.

"You will appear in TikTok videos with me!" Po Po announced.

"See, this is the reason I was given for our visit," Kelsey said.

"Um." He didn't want to be rude; he just had no idea how to respond.

"In some videos, I show off my cooking skills," Po Po said. "We will make a video where you show me how to cook something Korean, okay?"

"You can say no," Kelsey said. "It's really okay."

"No, it's not okay!" Po Po exclaimed. "This is the perfect idea. It will kill two birds with one rock. You will show Nicole how you are so kind to her grandma, and also that you can cook."

She did make a good point.

"And what do you get out of this?" he inquired.

"I learn to make Korean food, and I help you and Nicole get together." She nodded decisively. "It is a very good situation for me."

"Tell him the other reason, Po Po," Kelsey said.

"Because having a handsome man in my videos will make me

more popular! People love handsome men in cooking videos. It will be best if you take off your shirt."

Okay, David *really* didn't know how to respond to that.

He wished Nicole were here to run interference.

"Nicole has seen you without a shirt, hasn't she?" Po Po asked.

Dealing with a lecture hall full of nineteen-year-olds would be much easier than this.

"Po Po!" Kelsey said. "You're embarrassing him."

"It is not that *I* want to see you shirtless," Po Po continued. "It is just for my viewers. All for their sake. That is why I made the difficult decision to ask you. They enjoy the videos where I rate famous men, so I think they will like this."

"Are you going to rate me?"

"No, I will just say you are granddaughter's boyfriend."

"Please don't," he said, much as he enjoyed hearing himself referred to as Nicole's boyfriend. "Nicole won't like it."

"Fine. I will just say you are her special friend and wiggle eyebrows, okay?"

She seemed to take the fact that he was stunned into speechlessness—yet again—as acquiescence.

"Great!" she said. "We will make so many videos together."

"So many?"

"Yes, I think we should start today. We will go out for bungeoppang and Kelsey will film it. What do you think? When you come to my place tomorrow—"

"David might have plans," Kelsey said. "He has a job, you know."

"He can come after his job."

David nodded. "Tomorrow evening is fine, but I'm not taking off my shirt."

"Okay," Po Po said. "I will drink lots of coffee tomorrow so I can stay up late to make new content for TikTok."

"No," Kelsey said. "Last time you drank lots of coffee, you had a bad reaction."

Po Po gave her a dismissive look. "David, you will bring snacks from H-Mart and explain them to me, okay?"

"Okay," he said, feeling like he'd just been bulldozed by Nicole's *grandmother*.

"What will we make?" Po Po asked.

"Maybe galbitang?"

"I don't know what that is."

"Oh, I love galbitang," Kelsey said. "Good idea."

"You can buy all the ingredients and come to my house at seven," Po Po said. "I'm not sure what you need, and Kelsey is tired of driving me around, so I won't volunteer her for this." She reached up and touched his face.

"What are you doing?" Kelsey asked.

"Seeing how many grains of rice Nicole left in her bowl." Po Po located his small facial scar, from when he'd had chicken pox in kindergarten. "Just one, I guess."

"Po Po! Don't scare him off."

"Wah, he's not scared!" Po Po turned to David. "The number of leftover grains is how many pockmarks your husband will have. This was what we told children."

"Husband? This seems a bit premature," Kelsey said, grasping her grandmother's arm. "I think it's time we leave. See you tomorrow, David! I'm sure it'll be lots of fun."

Oh, dear. What was he getting himself into?

"You wear glasses?" Po Po asked as David studied the galbitang recipe he'd printed out. They were in her kitchen.

"Just for reading." He returned his attention to the recipe but could feel her studying him.

"I thought glasses were uncool. My daughter was very upset when she needed them in high school. But earlier, Kelsey showed me this Twitter thread—is that what it's called, even though it has nothing to do with sewing? It was all pictures of men wearing glasses, and women were going, how do you say, gah-gah over it?"

"David, I think she's trying to tell you to wear glasses for these videos," Kelsey said.

"Yes, this is exactly what I am saying. People will love it!" Po Po cackled with glee.

Well, he supposed he could do that.

After all, Nicole liked him in glasses, and it would amuse her.

"Professor Cho, I never thought I'd see the day!"

David's grad student walked into his office, holding up his phone, at the appointed time for their meeting to discuss his thesis.

But clearly Hunter had something else on his mind.

"You're famous!" Hunter said, then burst into laughter.

Alarmed, David nearly grabbed Hunter's phone from his hand.

"What are you talking about?" he asked instead, in a deliberately mild tone.

"Everyone thinks you're hot! This woman on Twitter is famous for all the pictures she posts of men wearing glasses, and she posted a video of you making food for your 'special friend's' grandmother."

Hunter held out his phone, and David looked at the video from Po Po and Kelsey's TikTok account. It had been retweeted thirty thousand times.

"Uh, right," David said. "Thanks for showing me. Now—"

"My sister didn't believe it when I said you were my supervisor."

"Right. How about—"

"And one of your undergrad students replied and said, 'That's my prof!'"

"Thanks for letting me know."

Hunter studied him for a moment. "Look, I'm sure it'll all blow over in a day or two. Stuff moves fast these days."

Yes, David would reassure himself with that, and he'd just hope that no one else he knew in person—other than Nicole—would find this.

Unfortunately, his hopes proved to be in vain.

22

"YOU HAVE A GIRLFRIEND?" Umma shouted over the phone. "And I had to learn this from an internet video?"

David had been about to order food for his Friday dinner with Nicole, but that would probably have to wait half an hour now. He couldn't imagine this call with his mother would take less than that.

"I don't have a girlfriend," he said.

"Then what else is a 'special friend'?"

"She lives next door to me. We're friends. That's all." He might wish for something else, but he wasn't going to say that now.

Umma sniffed. "Well, that's okay. I think you will have many women interested in you now. You should make a Twitter account and reply. You will have many dates. This is not how things worked in my day, but maybe..."

"No, I'm not creating a Twitter account." Actually, he'd created one about ten years ago to see what all the fuss was about but hadn't used it in ages.

"Okay, I will make a Twitter account and say you are my son and you live in Toronto. I will be your dating manager."

David was getting a headache. "Please don't."

"Don't you want to get married again?"

"Yes, but I can figure it out for myself."

"Can you? You've been single for four years. Or are you in love with this 'special friend'?"

He pinched the bridge of his nose. "Umma, I can take care of it."

Unsurprisingly, this wasn't enough to reassure his mother, and he spent another twenty-five minutes talking about his love life with her.

Nicole had been on her lunch break when Kelsey had sent her a text, telling her to look at their latest TikToks.

The videos were *hilarious*.

And now, as Nicole knocked on David's door, she was still in a good mood.

David, however, looked more tired than he usually did on Fridays, but he still smiled when he saw her, and his gaze lingered on her chest as she took off her coat.

"You're a star!" she told him.

"So I've heard," he said drily.

"I can't believe you agreed to make videos with my grandma."

"She was very persuasive. She paid me a surprise visit on Wednesday to ask for my help and threatened to have a medical emergency if I said no. I figured you could have a laugh at my expense, so why not?"

She couldn't help feeling touched. He seemed to care very much about making her laugh.

"But I didn't expect it to be so popular," he said. "I didn't expect my grad students and my mother to find it."

She laughed. "Your mother?"

"Yes."

"The problem," she said, wrapping her arms around his neck,

"is that you put on your glasses. I've told you how hot you look in those, haven't I?"

"Once your grandmother saw me with glasses, she insisted I wear them in the video."

She couldn't help laughing again. "Well, uh, thank you for satisfying her whims, but if you ever need help saying no to my family, just let me know."

She'd never thought a man appearing in her grandma's TikToks would warm her heart, but then again, she'd never been able to conceive of such a thing happening. Po Po's popularity on TikTok had definitely been one of the big surprises of the year.

And David, though he seemed slightly annoyed with the attention now, was just so agreeable. She'd make sure she treated him *very* well tonight so he'd forget all about this.

"What's for dinner?" she asked.

"About that," he said. "Due to the long phone conversation with my mom, in which she tried to involve herself in my dating life and start a Twitter account, I didn't order until fifteen minutes ago, so it'll be a little while."

"Where did you order from?"

"A Filipino restaurant near Bathurst and Wilson. Since I don't have a car, it's a bit inconvenient for me to pick up the food, so I got delivery."

"That's okay." She was hungry, but she could wait.

Unfortunately, her stomach could not. It protested. Loudly.

"Alright," David said, "how about we eat dessert first?"

"Why, Professor Cho," she said, "how scandalous!"

And with those words, she shimmied her body against his, and he made a growl in the back of his throat.

"What did you get for me?" she asked with a seductive wink.

"It's from the same bakery where I got the ube cake." He stepped away from her and opened a box, revealing what looked like two lemon tarts with a little dollop of meringue on top. "Calamansi tarts. Shall we eat them now?"

"I don't see how I can say no."

He slid each tart onto a plate and placed one at what was now "her" spot at the breakfast bar.

She had a bite. The tangy filling made her groan.

"Good?" he asked.

"What if I said no?"

He frowned. "Well, I guess I'd buy you an ube cake tomorrow to compensate. Or ensaymada. Those looked tasty, too. A kind of brioche, I think?"

Oh, God. Why was he making her heart melt? Having tea with her parents and sibling. Making videos and H-Mart trips with her grandmother. Buying her dessert every week.

He was so kind and considerate, and he would make a very nice boyfriend. There were tons of people drooling over him on social media.

He'll fall in love with someone else soon.

It felt like there was a countdown on their so-called arrangement. She didn't know when it would end…but it would. A man like this belonged in a relationship, and she did not—and besides, he'd given no indication he wanted anything else with her.

That's a good thing, she reminded herself.

She just couldn't bear to think of how it would end. The pain of him saying he'd met someone, the light in his eyes while talking about that woman.

"You're quiet," he said. "Do you really not like the tart? When you groaned, were you pretending? If so, I can eat your tart"—he pulled her plate toward him—"and then I'll buy you the cake tomorrow."

Okay, no. He wasn't getting away with this.

"Mine," she said, grabbing back her plate.

"Is that so?" He lifted up a forkful of her tart.

"David!" She couldn't believe he'd dare to do this.

But then he fed her the bite.

"Of course I wouldn't take the tart away from you," he

murmured. His breath on her cheek turned her on even more, and she made a show of licking her lips afterward.

And even though she ate her whole calamansi tart—and enjoyed it very much—the next day, there was a knock on her door, and she opened it to find not a person, but two pastries in a box. Ensaymada? They looked like they were topped with cheese.

She glanced down the hallway and saw the professor next door entering his unit.

She didn't suppress her smile.

23

THE FOLLOWING FRIDAY AFTERNOON, Nicole was at work when she got a most distressing text from David.

Sorry, I can't have dinner with you tonight. I'm sick. I stayed home from work today.

Oh, no! How awful.

That sucks, she replied. *What do you have?*

Bad cold, I think. I'm very tired.

Do you need anything from the pharmacy? she asked. *I can pick it up on the way home.*

Actually, if you could get some Advil and throat lozenges, that would be good. If you're sure it's not too much trouble.

Of course not.

She couldn't help feeling disappointed. Friday evening was the highlight of her week, and that wasn't entirely because of David, but still.

But more than anything, she felt terrible that he was sick.

I can pick up some food for you, too, she offered. *Is there some soup you'd like?*

Are you sure you don't mind? There's a place near us where you can get samgyetang. I'll find the link. You can get whatever you like from there, and I'll pay you back.

She started typing. *No worries! I want to look after you.*

She stared at the words on her phone, then deleted them.

You don't have to pay me back, she wrote instead. *This is my week to get dinner.*

She sent the message, put her phone away, and returned to work.

For the next hour, she worked efficiently, the thought of going home to David making her more productive than usual. She ordered the food before she left the office, then picked it up thirty-five minutes later. She quickly got the stuff from the pharmacy before heading to their building and knocking on David's door.

It took him longer than usual to answer. He wore pajama pants and a hoodie, and he looked awful. It pulled at something in her chest.

She went to hug him, but he stepped back.

"I don't want you to get sick," he said.

"Okay, no hugs, but I'm staying for dinner," she said firmly.

"Then I'll leave."

They sat down to eat. Nicole had gotten kimchi sujebi for herself. Samgyetang, which she'd never tried before, was ginseng chicken soup—a small whole chicken was stuffed with ginseng, garlic, rice, and other things. If he were well, she would have asked for a bite of his, but she shouldn't be sharing his germs now, and besides, she wasn't going to take soup from a sick person.

After dinner, she left so he could get some rest, making him promise to tell her if he needed anything. When she got to her apartment, she planned to watch a movie, but she couldn't fully relax.

David still had half the samgyetang, but what else would he eat tomorrow? Canned soup? Instant noodles?

Before she realized what she was doing, she was on the phone with her mom.

"Can you send me your recipe for jook?"

There were a few seconds of silence on the other end of the phone.

"Are you sick, Nicole? I can make it and bring it over for you."

"No, no, I'm fine."

"But you only eat jook when you're sick."

"I know, but..."

Oh, God. She could see the error of her ways now. It was just jook. Surely there were countless recipes online. Wasn't it basically just boiling rice with lots of water and chicken? Not that it had to have chicken, but that was how her mom always made it.

"You're cooking for David, aren't you?" Mom asked. "He's the one who's sick?"

"Yes," Nicole said sullenly. "It's for David. Don't you dare say this means—"

"Of course not. I would never suggest you have something other than friendly feelings for him. Who, me?"

"Mom, stop it. Will you give me the recipe or not?"

"Ah, you're so touchy. But the problem is that I don't have the recipe written down. I'll just have to explain it to you, okay?"

Ten minutes later, Nicole ended the call and massaged her temples.

What if David didn't like jook? She could text him, but then he'd say not to trouble herself. She should make something else, too, something she knew he liked. Like the short rib soup he'd cooked in the video with Po Po. Unfortunately, the exact recipe hadn't been posted, just brief instructions.

She texted her cousin. *Hey, do you have the galbitang recipe that David made last week? I want to cook it for him as a surprise.*

After sending the text, she cursed herself. Saying it would be "a surprise" would probably fuel everyone's thoughts about her feelings for David.

He's sick, she explained. *Whatever you do, don't tell Po Po, okay?*

A few minutes later, Kelsey sent Nicole the recipe and promised not to tell anyone that Nicole was cooking for her neighbor.

Nicole wasn't entirely sure she believed her cousin, but what could she do at this point? Besides, could her family really tease her more than they already did?

The answer was yes. It was always yes.

She pushed those thoughts aside and concentrated on making her grocery list for tomorrow. She had to go grocery shopping this weekend anyway, so it wasn't like she was going *that* out of her way for David. And she'd definitely keep some galbitang for herself. Plus, it was good for her to know how to make jook.

Yep, nothing more to it than that.

Saturday afternoon, David woke up from his two-hour nap still feeling like crap.

He was heading to the fridge to pour himself some orange juice and figure out what to do for dinner when his phone buzzed.

Hey, are you awake? Nicole asked. *I have something to give you.*

His head felt like it was full of cotton, but he managed to type out a reply. *I'm here.*

A couple of minutes later, there was a knock at his door. He opened it to reveal Nicole, who was carrying a big pot.

"Let me put this down and I'll go back to get the rest," she said.

The rest?

She returned a minute later with another big pot, and after setting this one down, she removed both of the lids.

One was galbitang.

The other looked like...dakjuk? It was definitely rice

porridge.

"You made all this for me?" His voice was hoarse because of his cold. Yes, must be the reason.

She shrugged as though it was no big deal.

But he knew Nicole didn't particularly enjoy cooking, though she was capable enough in the kitchen. She just enjoyed, well, eating. She wasn't the sort of person who was always giving other people homemade food. So, the fact that she'd done this for him...

And that was when he knew for sure.

His feelings for Nicole weren't going anywhere, and this gesture had given him hope. She must feel something for him, right? Even if she was adamant she didn't want a relationship?

Should he confess his feelings?

Not now, of course. He wasn't feeling well.

Except he no longer felt quite so ill.

Nicole seemed unsure of what to make of his silence, and she started filling it. "This is the recipe you used in the video." She pointed to the galbitang. "I had Kelsey give it to me." She pointed at the other pot. "This is jook with chicken."

"My mom made something similar when we were sick." He pulled out two bowls and a ladle. "Thank you. I wasn't sure what I'd eat for dinner."

"Why two bowls? Are you having both?"

Oh. "I thought you were going to stay, but you don't have to, of course, though it would be nice to have company." He attempted to bat his crusty eyelashes, and she laughed at him.

"Okay, I'll stay."

She dished out some jook for both of them. She looked very pretty today, as she always did. Unlike usual, however, he had no urge to jump her.

"It's is the first time I've made this." She dipped her spoon into her bowl. "When I told my mom why I needed the recipe, she teased me about you."

She'd put up with her mom's teasing because she wanted to make something for *him*.

"I was wondering," he said. "Louie is your mom's last name?"

She nodded.

"I'd never heard of that as a Chinese name before. I'd assumed your hyphenated last name was all from your dad's family."

"I don't think it's usually Romanized that way anymore. More often L-U-I, at least for people from Hong Kong? Our language—not that I speak it—is similar to Cantonese, and my family came here a long time ago. I think my great-great-grandfather was the first to come to Canada, but he couldn't bring his family over. Head tax and all that. My grandfather immigrated here in the early fifties."

"What about your grandmother?"

"She came a few years later. They didn't know each other in China, and she was essentially a mail-order bride. I always just accepted that, but later I wondered about the legalities. Like, my grandfather was supposedly sponsored by his uncle, but from what I've read, I don't see how a Chinese person would have been allowed to sponsor an adult nephew a few years after the Exclusion Act ended. And then my grandmother? I'm not sure how it all worked, and I'm afraid to ask, but I do know my grandma is a citizen now. Maybe our name was written that way to make it look less Chinese."

He wanted to learn all he could about her, but unfortunately, his brain was struggling to form coherent questions today, so he smiled at her instead.

"My parents came to Vancouver a couple of years before I was born," he said at last.

"Would you want to move back there?"

He shook his head. "My career is here. I have tenure. I'm not going anywhere and—" He started hacking and had to blow his nose again.

Which was unfortunate, as he was pretty sure this wasn't a

good way to seduce a woman. Not that he wanted to go to bed with Nicole now, but he wanted to nurture whatever feelings had made her cook for him today.

If she got sick, he'd cook for her as well. He wanted to look after her.

She left an hour later, and he had a shower—which refreshed him a little—and read before turning out the lights, much earlier than usual.

When he awoke a few hours later, around midnight, he felt more like himself, but it was as if he was waiting for something.

Midnight. On a Saturday.

Right. He'd often hear certain noises from his next-door neighbor at this time, although he hadn't heard them in a while.

But since he was indisposed, perhaps she'd seek the company of someone else tonight.

There was no noise coming from her apartment, though. Had she been sleeping with other people in the past two months? If so, he hadn't heard her. They'd never talked about being exclusive, and they weren't *together*, not like that. She'd be within her right to bring someone else to her bed—or to go to someone else's bed.

He didn't like the idea. He might have been turned on when he'd heard her before, but now, he would be jealous.

David stayed awake for an hour, and to his relief, there was no thumping and moaning next door. He flattered himself and wondered if she had no interest in anyone but him right now. After all, she'd made several meals worth of food for him and ate dinner with him every Friday.

At last, he drifted off with Nicole on his mind, and when he woke up, she was immediately on his mind again, and his brain was no longer as fuzzy as it had been yesterday.

Somehow, he'd try to make her his.

24

"Can I help you?" the older white lady asked David.

"Uh, no," he said. "Just looking. Thank you."

But he'd been "just looking" at the florist for the past fifteen minutes, and he still had to purchase dessert.

"Is this for a lady friend?" she asked, apparently not content to leave him alone. "Or a gentleman friend? It *is* the twenty-first century."

"Yes, for a woman." *A friend with benefits whom I want to be my girlfriend.*

After offering a few suggestions, she left him alone, and he returned to asking himself what the hell he was doing.

A couple of days ago, he'd texted Nicole to see if she'd like to go out for dinner rather than staying in. The only time they'd eaten outside of home was Valentine's Day, aka his birthday. Since they'd started having sex, they hadn't gone anywhere together. But he wanted it to seem more like a date.

She'd declined, saying they should just get takeout.

Then he'd figured he'd buy her flowers, maybe a nice bunch of peonies, and lay out his feelings while they ate dessert. He suspected Nicole was the kind of person who'd enjoy a bouquet of flowers on her counter.

Except when he'd walked into the florist and seen all the flowers, he'd realized a bouquet of roses or peonies might freak her out because of what they represented.

Yes, they'd been friends for a while, sleeping together for more than two months, but that still felt like it would be moving too fast.

Maybe something simpler, like daisies?

No, daisies didn't seem like the right kind of flower for Nicole. For some reason, he thought she'd like peonies. Big, showy flowers.

This whole plan was terrible.

There was no way he could see his confession of feelings going well when Nicole had made it abundantly clear what she wanted. She thought marriage would destroy her, whereas he wanted to get married again. She was afraid of losing her identity in a relationship.

Maybe the better approach would be to just continue to treat her well and prove that he wouldn't stop her from being who she was. That he was capable of giving her space when she needed it. Eventually, he would confess his feelings, and it would be easier for her to see that a relationship between them could work without her compromising herself.

Of course he didn't want her to be a different person for him. He liked her as she was.

He understood her concerns, but at the same time, she was different from who she'd been ten years ago; nobody would be able to treat her the same way without her having harsh words with them. She'd never get to the point of losing herself in a relationship again, especially when she was so worried about the possibility.

And, of course, he'd never behave like her ex.

By putting off his confession, was he being a wuss, or was he being sensible?

Sensible. Definitely sensible.

Yes, peonies would freak her out, so instead he'd get something else. Like the sex toy in the bottom of his dresser. He was positive an anal massager would be less frightening for Nicole than flowers.

And he found it rather delightful that this was true.

But.

He wished he could give her flowers, too.

Still, the sex toy was meaningful, even if it was more for him than her. It said, *I trust you.*

Satisfied, he was about to walk out of the florist and pick up their food, but then something caught his eye. A gift that could be cute and sweet, but he knew exactly what he'd pair it with, and that would make Nicole laugh.

Alright, he had a new plan for dessert.

Nicole felt guilty. Rose had texted her earlier, asking if she had plans for dinner. Rose never texted about getting together during the week, and if it weren't for David, Nicole would be happy to meet up. But she'd promised David she'd see him tonight, so she'd told Rose she was busy.

Last Friday, David had been sick. He'd felt better by Tuesday, but he'd also been busy marking exams, so she hadn't seen him since bringing him jook and galbitang, and she couldn't bear the thought of not seeing him today. He was supposed to order food from the Nicaraguan restaurant she liked, the food she'd originally planned to get last week before he'd asked her to get samgyetang.

Sure enough, when he opened the door and she smelled the delicious food, she couldn't help but smile. Also because *he* was here and she...missed him?

It had only been six days since she'd seen this guy. She shouldn't be missing him.

Must be because she was horny, that was all.

"How are you feeling?" she asked as she stepped inside.

He bent down and pressed a kiss to the base of her neck.

"Don't worry. I'm perfectly well." He gave her ass a dirty squeeze, and for a moment, she was tempted to drag him to the bedroom, but...

Carne asada. She needed to eat her carne asada first. And the sweet plantains. Those were her favorite. If David had gotten the wrong side dish, she'd be incredibly disappointed.

But, no. He'd gotten exactly what she'd asked for.

They sat down at the breakfast bar, and perhaps it was because they hadn't had sex in over a week, but she was particularly distracted by his body today. After her first bite of plantain, she placed her hand on his leg, her fingers gently stroking his inner thigh.

"How am I supposed to use a knife and fork when you're doing that?" he asked, even though he seemed to be eating his food without difficulty.

It took her longer to eat than usual because she kept touching him. Mmm. He really did have nice thighs, didn't he?

At last, she finished her meat, plantains, rice and beans, and vegetables, and David brought out dessert.

"That's dessert?" she asked.

"Well, one of them is. The other is a gift for you. Guess which is the real succulent."

It wasn't hard to figure out, but the pastry succulent was still pretty life-like. It came in a clear plastic container with layers of colorful "sand" that were obviously edible. The "succulent" was a funny-shaped macaron.

"What flavor is it?" she asked.

"Matcha and white chocolate."

She turned her attention to the real succulent in its little terracotta pot.

"I thought it would be funny to get a real one, too," he said.

She picked up a small spoon and dipped it into the creamy layers of the dessert. "Mmm. Are we sharing this, or do you have your own?"

"That was the last of its kind. I have this instead." He set a plate in front of him.

"That looks depressingly ordinary."

"It's banana, coconut, and chocolate. I'm sure it'll be good."

She helped herself to a big bite.

"Hey!" he said, then reached to try some of hers.

She moved it out of the way and shoved the succulent—the real succulent—in front of him. He stilled before his spoon hit the dirt.

"I'm kidding," she said. "You bought this delicious treat for me. You deserve to try a tiny bite."

"Your bite was hardly tiny."

She shrugged and gave him a coy look over her shoulder.

He took a small bite, and she watched as the spoon slid between his lips.

Oh, God.

The first time she'd seen David, she hadn't been attracted to him, but now she didn't understand how that was possible. What had her former self been thinking?

As soon as they were both finished their desserts, she kissed him.

"I can't wait to have my way with you," she said.

The next thing she knew, her shirt was on the floor, and David's arms were around her. How had that happened so fast?

He backed her against the wall by the door and kissed her hard, holding her arms above her head. She might not be able to touch him with her hands, but she could roll her hips against his and feel him hardening.

She grinned at her good fortune.

She'd wanted a partner for sex so she didn't have to find someone new all the time, and she'd found the perfect one, right next door.

But one day he'll...

Luckily, what David said next wiped those thoughts from her mind.

"I bought something for you to use in bed."

"Oh?" She already had tons of sex toys, but she could always use more. "Another candy cane dildo?"

"No." He smiled. "It's for you to use...on me."

He let go of her hands, and she followed him into the bedroom. He removed something from the bottom drawer in his dresser. She'd never seen one before, but she was pretty sure she knew what it was.

"A remote-controlled prostate massager?"

He nodded.

"Ooh, I was curious about these. Have you played with it by yourself?"

He nodded again.

She pictured David stroking himself, then lubing this up and slipping it into his ass.

"I always—well, by 'always,' I mean for over a decade—wanted to try using one with someone," he said. "But I never..."

The fact that he felt so comfortable with her was stirring up *feelings*.

She couldn't have that, so she started undressing him instead. Once she'd unbuttoned his shirt and tossed it on the ground, she stroked her hands over his lean chest and admired the curve of his back—she'd never found a man's back quite so sexy before. She reached for the button on his pants just as he started pushing down hers. She quickly removed his underwear, then her own, desperate to get naked with him.

When she jumped onto the bed, he followed her, and then

they were kissing; she was practically riding his leg because she couldn't seem to help herself.

He slid down her body and parted her folds. He slipped two fingers inside her at the same time as he started licking her, and she couldn't help bucking against his face. He suckled her clit before running his tongue over her entrance... She was losing track of what he was doing now, but it didn't matter, all that mattered was that he was making her feel so good...

She cried out as she gripped the sheet in her hands.

He smiled up at her, her moisture on his lips. Fuck, he looked good like that.

"Your turn." She pushed him onto his back before taking his cock in her mouth.

Yes, he had a lovely cock, and she loved pleasuring him. She sucked on him eagerly—but not for long. There was something else she wanted to try.

She released him and reached into his night table. She knew where he kept his lube, but she'd never used it for this purpose.

"Turn over," she murmured.

He rolled onto his stomach, his arms crossed under his head, and she ran her hands up and down his back before giving his ass a good squeeze. He had a great ass, too.

"Can I touch you here first?" she asked.

"Yes."

She lubed up her finger and slowly circled his hole before sliding inside. She'd never done this with a guy before. When she moved her finger in just a little farther, he made an incoherent noise, and she couldn't help how excited that made her.

After playing with him for a few minutes, she grabbed the toy. She wondered how David had chosen this specific one, if he'd gone to a store or ordered it online.

She put on a copious amount of lube, then slowly began pushing it inside him.

"That's it," she murmured. "You can take it."

She thrust it gently in and out of him before lying next to him and picking up the remote. She studied the settings for a moment. There were a bunch of vibration patterns and intensities.

Nicole turned it to low, constant vibration and began lazily stroking his cock again.

He hissed out a breath and gritted his teeth.

"What's it like?" she asked.

"It's…different. I…ahh."

She'd turned up the intensity and changed the setting to slow pulsation.

God, she was going to have so much fun with this. She liked it when he couldn't form full sentences.

And to think, she'd once imagined sex with David would be boring!

Perhaps he thought she was a little too self-satisfied, because he turned toward her and slipped his hand between her legs. His finger disappeared inside her pussy. He adjusted the position of his hand so his palm pressed against her clit, and when she looked at the toy coming out of his ass, she came.

"David," she said, "do you think you could wear that while we have sex?"

"That was my hope."

She turned him onto his back, and he bent his legs. After rolling a condom on his erection, she raised her body above him and slowly lowered herself. The head of his cock split her apart, and he was inside her.

Oh, God, he was inside her.

Though this was far from the first time, it was still almost overwhelming.

She adjusted the prostate massager to rapid pulsation.

"Are you trying to kill me?" he muttered.

Nicole left it like that for a few seconds before turning it back to the previous setting. She held the remote in her hand as she bounced on his cock.

His gaze was intense on hers, and sweat beaded on his brow. He grabbed her hips and helped her move up and down.

It was almost too much to look at him, but somehow, she couldn't look away.

"Nicole, I..."

She'd seen David come many, many times, but today, he came with a force she'd never seen before, and if someone were in her bedroom next door, they'd definitely hear. She turned off the prostate massager when it seemed like he was finished, but then he jerked into her one last time, and that pushed her over the edge. She collapsed on his chest.

After they cleaned up, their need to continue touching each other was stronger than usual. Nicole curled up next to David, her head on his chest.

For some reason, she couldn't help thinking of the painting in her closet. He might like it and not think any less of her for it.

Before she could second-guess herself, she jumped up, got dressed, hurried to her apartment, and retrieved the painting.

"Is that...?" he began when she returned to his bedroom.

"Yes, I had someone do a pin-up painting of me. I know it's vain to spend money on such a thing, and I'm too embarrassed to hang it up, but..." She started to regret showing him, but when she moved to turn it around, he stopped her.

"I think it's amazing," he said. "Very sexy."

"The artist is talented, isn't she?"

He nodded. "You look incredible—it looks just like you, and I like the way the skirt is flying up. I'd love to see this every day, and I love that you were confident enough to get it done. I bet you enjoyed posing for it."

"I did."

She breathed out a sigh of relief. He wasn't being weird and judgmental about this.

But as she undressed and settled back into bed, she couldn't help feeling agitated.

She trusted him and felt so damn close to him, and this wasn't what she wanted. She couldn't lie to herself and claim it was just sex.

No, the sheer terror she felt made it impossible.

Terror that he'd find someone else. That a month from now, someone else would use that toy on him. Someone else would receive a cute succulent and a cute succulent dessert.

And *those* feelings terrified her. It was a vicious loop.

She hadn't had such feelings for a decade, but David was special.

She couldn't have more with him, though.

First of all, because she couldn't imagine him wanting it. It ran counter to her experiences in the last ten years. Second of all, because relationships had not been good to her in the past.

"Is something wrong?" David asked drowsily.

She sifted her fingers through his hair. "Don't worry. I'm fine."

"You sure?"

A moment later, his breathing changed. He was asleep.

But she was wide awake. This was becoming too much, and she had to protect herself. Extricate herself from this situation before it was too late. She should stop seeing him so often.

Except how could she possibly give up Fridays?

No, she wouldn't, but she'd stop visiting him at other times during the week, and she'd try to text him as little as possible.

The ache in her chest?

It was just proof that this was the right thing to do.

25

NICOLE STARED at Sierra's plate. Why did her friend order Brussels sprouts nearly every time they came to Ossington Cider Bar? True, the sprouts were covered in cheese and bacon, but still.

Nicole's stomach growled, but not because she was tempted by the Brussels sprouts. She suddenly realized she hadn't eaten since noon, which wasn't like her.

She didn't want a burger or mussels, though. Maybe she'd just get a brownie with ice cream. That was a solid dinner, wasn't it?

"Nicole?" Rose said softly.

Nicole jerked her head up. "Yeah? Did you say something?"

"I just asked if you're okay," Rose said. "You're a bit spaced out."

Nicole had a sip of her blackberry nectarine cider, which didn't taste as good as it normally did. "I'm fine." She managed a smile. "Long week at work, you know?"

Victor and Mike weren't here today. It was just the five of them: Nicole, Sierra, Rose, Charlotte, and Amy.

"It's that guy next door, isn't it?" Amy bounced in her seat. "Wouldn't it be cool if you married the guy next door, like me?"

Nicole nearly spat out her cider. "*Marry?* I'm not marrying anyone. And I don't like him. Not in that way."

"Sure, sure," Sierra said skeptically.

Last time, Nicole's slowness to respond had made them suspicious, but this time, her quick denial seemed to have the same effect. Apparently, they'd assume she liked David romantically no matter what she said and how she said it. It was horribly unfair.

She was tired of denying it when her friends were never going to believe her anyway, so she said, "Fine, I like him a little, okay?"

"You sound as cranky as me," Charlotte muttered.

Just then, Charlotte's sister Julie, their server tonight, came around. "Who's cranky?"

"Nicole," Charlotte said. "She has a crush on a guy."

"Can you get me a warm brownie with ice cream?" Nicole asked Julie. "And another of these." She held up her pint glass, which was still half-full, but she intended to drink the rest of it in the next five minutes. "Thank you."

"Coming right up," Julie said before heading to another table.

Rose sipped her drink. "Nicole even declined to go out for dinner with me yesterday. I wanted to try a new Taiwanese restaurant, but—"

"I'd already made plans with David," Nicole said, "and I really wanted sweet plantains."

"Or maybe one particular plantain?" Sierra waggled her eyebrows.

Nicole ignored that. "Plus, he'd been sick, so I only got to see him briefly last Friday, though I did make him jook the next day."

Dammit, why had she said that?

"You cooked for him," Rose said. "Interesting."

"Can we move on to another topic?"

"What did you have for dessert yesterday? He always gets you nice desserts, doesn't he?"

"He got me a matcha and white chocolate pastry with a

macaron on top. It looked like a potted succulent. He also brought me a real succulent to go with it."

"He likes you. He definitely likes you."

Nicole couldn't help being hopeful, but she quickly shoved that feeling away. In her annoyance, she almost shot back, *What do you know about such things?*

Luckily, she managed to bite her tongue. Rose didn't deserve that.

"I agree," Amy said. "He bought you a cute plant. That has to mean something, and unlike cut flowers, it'll last. Isn't that sweet?"

"He probably wanted to get you flowers," Charlotte said, "but figured you'd freak the fuck out, so he got you a succulent instead."

"He just did it because of the pastry," Nicole protested. "It was a little joke, that's all."

"You sure spend a lot of time together. I doubt you'd do that if you didn't both like each other. Mind you, I don't enjoy spending much time with people in general, so maybe I'm not the best one to give advice. But Mike doesn't really count as a person."

"Um…"

"That's a positive thing! Like, it's easier to be with him than other people."

"Yeah, it's like that with David, too," Nicole admitted. "I can relax. I don't have to constantly worry about what he'll say or how he'll react to every little thing I do."

Thankfully, her brownie arrived. Amy eyed it hungrily, but no way was Nicole sharing. Amy could get her own damn brownie.

Ugh, what was happening to her? Nicole was usually cool and self-possessed, and now she was shoveling brownie into her mouth and trying not to think about the man who'd given her a succulent last night. She just wanted to go back to who she used to be.

But what if that woman was gone?

"You should say something to him," Amy said, "I'm positive it'll go well."

"No." Nicole stabbed her brownie angrily, even though the poor brownie had never done anything to hurt her. "You don't understand. Men never feel that way about me. I'm the woman they fuck before they find true love, and don't tell me otherwise. It's happened many times."

"That's just bad luck. You think you don't deserve it?" Rose asked.

"Of course not! I'm awesome." Nicole didn't feel awesome right now, though. She was whiny, and she hated it.

"Exactly." Rose nodded. "If David has good taste, he should see that, too."

Her friends were kind, but what did it matter?

On the off chance David had feelings for her, it wasn't like Nicole was going to date him. She wasn't putting herself through that shit again. She'd done it before and learned her lesson.

Life was better this way.

Except she used to love coming home to an empty apartment with no one to make demands on her, and eating whatever she wanted in front of the TV. She used to love seeing a cute guy at the bar and flirting with him. And now, those things made her lonely and tired.

"By the way," Charlotte said, "I saw David in your grandma's TikTok videos."

"He did what?" Amy was nearly shouting in Nicole's ear.

"Yeah." Nicole sighed. "My grandma asked him to make food with her and appear in her videos because apparently handsome men can make videos more successful. Who knew."

"He must really like you if he appeared in your *grandma's* TikToks."

Nicole shrugged. "He's a nice guy."

"You know who you sound like?" Charlotte asked, then continued without waiting for an answer. "Me. When I confessed to having teeny-tiny feelings for Mike. You're putting up such a fuss. Remember how much you teased me back then?"

Nicole responded by drinking more cider. "I apologize. I can understand now how annoying it is."

Her friends looked around the table, and by silent agreement, seemed to decide to change the topic.

"Any plans for the summer?" Amy asked, upbeat.

But although the conversation moved on, Nicole's thoughts did not.

Sunday afternoon, Nicole was moping around her apartment, trying to stop herself from texting David or going to H-Mart to buy more delicious snack food. She'd just about lost her willpower when the phone rang. It was her grandma.

"Wah, who does she think she is? How dare she?"

Oh, no. What family drama had Nicole missed now?

"Did Kelsey try to stop you from climbing a ladder again?" Nicole inquired, thinking back to the last time she'd gotten a call like this. "Did she set out plastic cockroaches for you to smack with your wok?"

Po Po kept talking as though Nicole hadn't spoken. "I work so hard. I even did my hair special for yesterday's video."

"Yes, I saw that. You looked very nice."

"But nobody cares about me anymore. All they care about is *her*. She thinks she's so special, just because she is a hundred years old and can still dance. Aiyah, her dance moves are terrible!"

Nicole was confused. "Can you put Kelsey on the phone, please?"

There was a bunch of crashing and banging on the other end, but eventually she heard Kelsey's voice.

"Po Po has found her nemesis," Kelsey said. "There's an elderly

Korean lady who dances to K-pop and makes her own costumes, and one of her videos went viral. Po Po is jealous because Mrs. Lee is getting so much attention."

"She is stealing my thunder!" Po Po said. "Evil thunder stealer! How dare she!"

Nicole couldn't stop laughing. "I still care about you, Po Po."

"I want the whole world to love me! Be famous. You are just one person."

"Just one person? I'm your eldest grandchild."

"Fine. You are okay—"

"And there are still lots of views of your videos," Nicole said. "Lots of comments. You're doing pretty well. Mrs. Dong doesn't even have a single video online, does she?"

"I don't care about Mrs. Dong anymore."

"I thought she was your closest friend or dearest enemy. I was never quite sure."

"I need to go to Seoul and challenge Mrs. Lee to dance-off!"

"Um… Po Po, you're not a very good dancer."

"But she is even worse! She has no skills. People are just impressed because she is so old. When you get to one hundred years, anything you do is impressive," Po Po scoffed. "You ask David to take me to Korea, okay? He speaks the language, yes? He will be translator."

"Po Po, don't you think this is a bit extreme?"

"I saw a Popsicle—"

"Listicle."

"—yesterday, and she was on it, and I wasn't. If you won't let me follow my dreams—"

"I think it's great that you and Kelsey are doing these TikToks but—"

"Then do me a favor. Ask David if he will star in another video with me. Also ask if he has three handsome friends who will take off their shirts and be my back-up dancers."

Nicole collapsed on the couch in laughter.

"Why are you laughing?" Po Po demanded. "I need to get ahead of Mrs. Lee. What else do you suggest? Ask David."

"No. He just made videos with you a couple of weeks ago, and he has to submit the final marks for his classes. He's busy."

"Did you have a fight?"

"No."

"What is wrong? You sound weird."

"I do not sound weird," Nicole said, trying her hardest to sound normal, even though, yes, okay, fine, she was a tiny bit sad at the thought of David. She wanted to see him today, but it would be better to keep her distance.

"You will make up—"

"I told you. We didn't have a fight. And we're not dating."

"—and then you will ask him in a few weeks. He will say yes."

"We'll see," Nicole said.

"Fine. Do not help your poor old po po."

"I can help you in other ways, but please, no more surprise visits."

Twenty minutes later, Nicole finally managed to get off the phone. A part of her wanted tell David about that phone call—when had he become the person she wanted to tell about everything? Ugh.

Instead, she'd make herself some coffee and try not to look forward to Friday…or fantasize about getting stuck in the elevator again with him.

Yep, she needed to reign in these feelings ASAP.

~

"Saturday evening," Murray said by way of greeting. "You free?"

"Should be," David said, looking up from his spreadsheet.

"Now, I don't want to spring this on you as a surprise like Cassie."

Oh, no. Murray was going to—

"Our daughter has a friend at work who's a little older than her—a little younger than you—and she's looking to settle down."

Yes, it was exactly as David had feared.

"Uh, sorry," he said. "I'm sure she's very nice, but I'm not interested. You see, the woman who lives next to me…"

David spent a few minutes describing how he and Nicole had gotten stuck in the elevator together, and how they'd started having dinner together on Fridays, and how they'd begun… making out. He made no mention of hearing her having sex. He also explained that Nicole had made it clear she didn't want a relationship, and his plan was to continue to treat her well and hope she would come to see him as someone who loved her and wouldn't make her change who she was.

Murray shook his head. "I think you're being a scaredy-cat."

David had been afraid of that.

"You've been seeing lots of this woman for months," Murray said. "You've already shown her who you are. Do you think another few months will really make a difference? Tell her now, and I bet she'll say yes. Don't be one of these people who's secretly in love with someone for years, like my brother. You have to seize the day!"

"You really think she'll say yes?"

"From all the time she's spent with you? From the food she made when you were sick? Yeah, I think this woman has feelings for you, too."

Well, it was nice to have someone reassure him.

But did Murray really know what he was talking about, or was he just being an encouraging friend? He'd never met Nicole, after all, and he had no recent experience with the dating world.

Still, even though David's hands were already shaking at the thought, he resolved to do something soon. This Friday.

And he knew exactly how he'd do it.

[26]

ANOTHER WEEK of work was over.

For some reason, this week had seemed particularly long, but now it was Friday. Nicole had ordered sushi, which should be delivered around seven.

Until then, she'd kick back and relax.

She changed into more comfortable clothes, and she was examining her small collection of wine when there was a knock on the door.

Was it David? He was early today.

She couldn't help smiling as she sauntered to the door and opened it up.

Indeed it was David, with a box in his hands. What had he brought for dessert?

But she couldn't think about that for long because the man himself looked particularly delectable. He was wearing khakis and a button-down shirt that was a nice shade of blue.

And they still had another forty minutes until food arrived.

"Hey." She took the box from his hands and set it on the counter, and then she pulled him down for a kiss.

Mmm. Why did he always taste so good?

She wrapped a leg around him and tried to climb him, but when she swept her tongue into his mouth, he put his hands on her shoulders and stepped away from her.

"Not yet," he said. "I have something to tell you."

Oh, gosh. He wasn't smiling at all.

"Is something wrong?" she asked.

He shook his head. "I thought we could have dessert first."

Okay. But something was definitely wrong. She could feel it.

David went to the counter and opened up the box. He took out a small ube cake, just like the one he'd bought on her birthday. That was sweet of him.

Then he stuck two candles in the cake, and her blood ran cold.

They weren't ordinary birthday candles. No, they were sticks with pink wax hearts, the wicks on top of the hearts.

He pulled out a lighter and lit them.

"Nicole." He took her hands in his. "I've very much enjoyed the time we've spent together, both in and out of bed, but I want more. I want to go on proper dates and say sappy things and talk about our future." He paused. "To be honest, I had my doubts when you wanted to be friends with benefits, because I already had a crush on you. I told myself I could do what you wanted, but it turns out I can't. You're amazing, and I love you."

Nicole was speechless.

"You're serious?" she said at last.

"Of course. I wouldn't say those things if I wasn't."

She couldn't help it; she burst into hysterical laughter, even though she knew this was the wrong reaction. "I'm sorry. It's just…this has never happened before."

"So, what do you think?"

"Men never feel this way about me." Rather, they stopped fucking her so they could confess their love to other women.

David took out a familiar note, one she'd given him months ago.

Here's your share, followed by a little heart.

Oh, God. Oh, God.

He'd kept it all this time.

As she stared at the note and the heart-shaped candles flickering on the cake, she tried to compose herself and avoid any more inappropriate reactions.

It was difficult, though, when she was so unfamiliar with such situations.

This was what she'd wanted, wasn't it? For someone to fall for her? Just to know it was possible?

Not David, though.

Never David.

Because the last thing she wanted was to break his heart.

They would have to stop seeing each other every Friday and sleeping together. They would just politely nod at each other in the hall. She'd have to be quiet when she had sex in her bed—she wouldn't want him to hear.

She couldn't stand to look at those blasted candles, so she blew them out.

"David," she said gently, "you know why I don't want a relationship."

He nodded. "I know you've had bad experiences in the past, and I know you're afraid of losing who you are, but I would never let that happen. I would support you and give you the space you need. When we live together, we'd make sure to get a two-bedroom place."

She just stared at him. He was talking about living together.

"Sorry," he said, scratching the back of his head. "That was moving too fast. But I promise, I wouldn't be like him. That's the last thing I want for you. We can figure out how to make this relationship work. It wouldn't have to be a lot different from what it is now."

No, he was wrong. It would be very different.

The idea of a relationship made her feel like she was chained to her bed, and she didn't like being restrained. She gripped the counter, feeling like the walls were already closing in on her.

She was supposed to be a confident, independent woman, but she'd always been a little soft and vulnerable on the inside, like her teenage self who'd wanted to be assured that everything wasn't her fault.

And now Nicole was a blubbering mess. She half wanted to yell at him, but she couldn't. He was too damn sweet and nice.

"Why did you ruin it?" she whispered. "What we had...it was exactly what I wanted."

David handed her a tissue. "I thought you might have feelings for me, too, based on some of the things you've said and done. Don't get me wrong," he added hastily, "I'm not saying you led me on. I just figured you might feel the same way, but if you don't—"

"I don't." The words tasted horrible in her mouth. They tasted...almost like a lie? But that was foolishness. There was no lie.

"Okay," he said. "I can't have dinner with you tonight. It would be too hard for me."

"I'm sorry," she whispered.

"If you don't want all the food yourself, you can leave my half outside my door and I'll pay you back for it. You can keep the cake."

He plucked the candles out of the cake and left.

An hour later, Nicole had eaten lots of sushi. She was now drinking red wine and eating dessert. Every bite reminded her of David, and it tasted like ash, but dammit, she wouldn't let cake go to waste.

Though she might feel miserable now, she was determined to become fabulous again. She'd go out and have fun. She made decent money, and she didn't have to answer to anyone. It was a good life.

But is it really, if I have to keep reminding myself...

Yes, it was. This life was a million times better than the one she'd had with Calvin.

She swallowed more wine. She shouldn't be in such a foul mood. Maybe she needed a nice orgasm to relax her and take the edge off.

Except her sex toys would remind her of David. How unfair.

She wondered if he'd eaten the sushi she'd left in front of his door. She'd texted to tell him it was there, but he hadn't replied.

It would be a crime to leave sushi in the hallway. She'd better make sure he'd taken it.

She tiptoed out to the hall—why was she acting like this was a top-secret mission?—to check. The food was gone.

What was he doing now? Was he wearing those sexy glasses and reading?

Would he get over her quickly?

She hoped he would.

She returned to her wine and ube cake. She would enjoy the hell out of this cake, dammit.

Nicole Louie-Edwards wasn't heartbroken, not one bit.

27

IN A CRUEL TWIST OF FATE, Nicole saw David on Monday.

She'd just checked her mail after work and was waiting by the elevators when someone approached.

David nodded at her, nothing more.

She hoped the elevator would come soon. Not because it was cruel that *she* had to wait for the elevators with him. No, her concern was only for him.

She was fine. Yes, she was.

The elevator mercifully came quickly, and they both stepped on. When the doors closed, they both stood facing forward. She could tell he was looking forward because she snuck a peek at him out of the corner of her eye.

At the twelfth floor, the elevator came to a sudden stop, and the doors didn't open.

Just her luck.

Well, it was bad luck for him, more than anything. Being stuck on an elevator with the woman he loved who didn't love him back. Must be awkward. For her, it was only a slight delay in when she got to take off her bra and eat instant noodles. No big deal. She was fine.

David stepped closer to her, and her heart sped up, even though he probably just wanted to press the emergency call button.

But before he could do so, the elevator started moving again, and she let out a sigh of relief, then held her breath until the elevator reached their floor.

They walked off and headed to their respective doors, and when Nicole closed the door behind her, a wave of anguish overtook her.

God, she hated that things weren't the same between them anymore, that they hadn't been able to have an easy conversation on the elevator, that he wasn't pushing her against the wall right now and kissing her. She yearned to be touched by him. In comfort, in desire...however he wanted to touch her.

She wrapped her arms around herself and squeezed her eyes shut.

Maybe she wasn't okay after all.

The following Saturday was Po Po's eighty-seventh birthday, and so they were out for lunch at Congee Princess. Nicole had never been here before, but it was the restaurant that Charlotte went to with her parents whenever they were in town.

There were seven of them clustered at a round table in the busy restaurant: Nicole, Po Po, Kelsey, Mom, Dad, Cam, and Cam's partner, Tessa.

"Why didn't you invite David?" Mom asked.

Nicole wasn't in the mood for this. She served herself some scallops to delay her answer.

"Wah, didn't you hear?" Po Po said. "They broke up."

Nicole jerked her head toward her grandmother. "What?"

"How come she knows and I don't?" Mom demanded.

"She likes me better than you." Po Po lifted her nose in the air. "I am cooler."

"Po Po!" Kelsey said. "Stop lying."

"David and I couldn't break up," Nicole said wearily, "since we were never together."

"This is...what do you call it?" Po Po said. "A technicality. I visited him on Tuesday."

"You *what*?" Nicole exclaimed. A few people in the restaurant looked in her direction, but mercifully, it was too loud in here for this to be much of a scene. Still, she lowered her voice. "You have no sense of boundaries."

"Boundaries? What are boundaries?"

Kelsey shook her head. "We had a long talk about this, Po Po. You're being obtuse."

"What is this word? I don't know it."

"You literally looked it up in the dictionary yesterday."

"Did I? But I am old. Bad memory. Who are you?"

"Don't joke about that." Kelsey turned to Nicole. "I refused to drive Po Po to your building on Tuesday, so she took a cab. She visited David because she wanted him to be in more videos, and also because she's somehow convinced he knows three hot men with six-packs—"

"Eight-packs!" Po Po interrupted.

"—who would be willing to dance shirtless in her videos."

Poor Tessa was just looking around the table, mouth hanging open, like she had no idea what to make of any of this.

Yeah, welcome to our family.

Cam whispered something to Tessa.

"Anyway, he politely refused," Kelsey said. "She kept badgering him, but he stayed firm—good for him. But then she demanded he take her to H-Mart and said he should ask his *girlfriend* to come along. When he told her, once again, that Nicole wasn't his girlfriend, Po Po said he should ask her to be his girlfriend, and he said that he had, but Nicole had declined...

Anyway, it went something like that, assuming Po Po wasn't lying to me."

Mom turned to Nicole. "You declined? What's wrong with him? Is it because he's divorced?"

"Nothing's wrong with David. He's great."

"So? I know you care for him. You made jook when he was sick."

"Yeah, so what?" Nicole said irritably.

"You also made him galbitang," Kelsey added.

"Why didn't I know about this?" Po Po shouted.

Mom ignored the outburst. "You do really like him, don't you?"

Nicole slumped in her chair. She was tired of lying to herself. Tired of lying to other people. "Yeah. I do like him."

Po Po grabbed Kelsey's phone. "I will call him and tell him that!"

"Ma, no!" Mom jumped up and grabbed the phone from Po Po, then put the phone on her chair and sat on it.

"Ah, you are stealing my moves," Po Po said. "Are you going to butt-dial him?"

"Can you please try *not* to scare Tessa off?" Cam muttered.

"Hello?" said a low, unfamiliar voice. "Kelsey?"

Nicole looked around, then realized the voice was coming from her mother's ass.

"Auntie!" Kelsey shrieked. "You butt-dialed someone and put it on speakerphone."

Mom picked up the phone and looked at the screen. "Who's Gerald?"

"Uh, I'm the guy on the other end of the phone."

Mom handed the phone back to Kelsey, who took it off speakerphone and whispered, "I'm so sorry. I'll text you later, okay?"

Po Po crossed her arms over her chest. "You better do some explaining. Who is this Gerald person? You live with me. You owe me answers! Is he a boyfriend?"

"Ma!" Mom said. "If you want Kelsey to keep living with you and doing chores and driving you around, you can't be so intrusive. Boundaries, remember."

"Hmph."

"And don't call David, either. Nicole admitted she likes him. How about we let her figure this out on her own, okay?"

Nicole nodded at her mother gratefully.

Once upon a time, Mom wouldn't have responded like this. It was hard to predict exactly what Mom might have done, but perhaps she would have told Nicole that she only had herself to blame for her bad experiences with love; they'd happened because she hadn't been positive enough. Nicole had feared telling her mother anything, but now, things were better.

"So, what about Mrs. Lee?" Mom asked Po Po.

Good. She was changing the subject.

"I don't care about Mrs. Lee anymore," Po Po said with a dismissive gesture.

"I thought she was stealing your thunder?"

"But TikTok is not the most important thing in life. This is new lesson I have learned. I was becoming too obsessed with it."

"What brought this about?" Mom asked.

"Mrs. Dong is in the hospital."

"Oh, no. What happened?"

"She broke hip. She forgot her keys and locked herself out, but she remembered she had left living room window open. So, she tried to climb through window but had an accident. I guess this is a bad thing to do when you are octopus."

"I think you mean 'octogenarian,'" Kelsey said. "And don't you dare try to climb through any windows. Why didn't she call one of her kids or grandkids instead?"

"She was too embarrassed to admit she forgot her keys. Kelsey took me to the hospital to see her, and even though I always talk about outliving her, I realized how sad I will be without her. So, I think it's more important for me to spend time with her than to be on more Popsicles than Mrs. Lee." Po Po turned to Nicole and shook her finger. "But if David changes his mind, I am still interested, okay? He can be in my videos and bring his friends."

Nicole nodded. "Okay."

Po Po helped herself to more food. "How about Gerald, Kelsey? Would he like to be in videos with me?"

Nicole returned her attention to her plate, then thought of something to ask Cam. But her sibling and Tessa had their heads bent together, and Cam was smiling. It made Nicole ache for David. To have him with her at family gatherings. To go home with him afterward.

God, she really did love him, didn't she?

She thought about him as they finished their meal, and even though everyone had eaten more than enough food, Kelsey had arranged for a special chocolate cake with candles to be served by the unsmiling waitress. Kelsey passed out party hats and filmed as they all sang "Happy Birthday" to Po Po.

And when everyone clapped, Nicole had a strange sensation in her chest. It was partly caused by her feelings for David—but not only by that.

"You okay?" Cam whispered.

"Yeah," Nicole said, even though she wasn't sure.

The plan had been to go to Ossington Cider Bar, as usual, but at the last minute, Sierra suggested L instead. Colton wasn't going to be there, but he'd encouraged her to use one of his credit cards and do something nice with her friends.

Nicole wasn't complaining. She could always eat more chocolate mousse and cheese.

They sat in a different place than last time, thank God—those chairs had been uncomfortable. Nicole was on the bench seating, between Rose and Charlotte, and once she'd drunk half her second dark chocolate espresso and orange martini, she finally worked up the courage to say what she wanted to say.

"I love David."

She immediately stuffed some sheep's cheese in her mouth and looked around at her friends. Not a single one of them looked surprised.

"You're not going to say 'I told you so'?" she asked. "After all the teasing you did?"

"We promised not to tease you anymore," Rose said, squeezing Nicole's hand. "What are you going to do? Will you tell him?"

Nicole drained her martini. "He already confessed his love to me with an ube cake and heart candles, and I turned him down."

"But *why*?"

"First of all, because I didn't realize how much I liked him at the time. And second of all, because I haven't had a relationship in a decade, and that was a terrible experience. I lost who I was, and I let him walk all over me. I don't want that to happen again."

"I can't imagine you letting someone walk all over you now," Amy said. "If that happens, you'll kick his ass, right? We can help."

"Don't volunteer me for shit without asking my permission," Charlotte muttered. "But, Nicole, from the little you've said about this guy, he doesn't sound anything like Calvin."

"He's not," Nicole admitted.

She forced herself to think more about being with David, really being with him. Maybe it was partly the booze and being surrounded by her friends—and the fact that some time had passed—but she could do it now without panicking.

David was a respectful man, and he wasn't dating a much younger woman because nobody else would put up with his crap. And unlike last time, she wasn't a lot younger, just six years instead of eighteen. It felt like they were at about the same place in their lives.

Also unlike Calvin, David was excellent in bed. Nicole had a lot to compare him to, and he was definitely better than average.

Even though he was kind and polite outside the bedroom, he could be pretty naughty when they were alone, and not at all afraid to explore new things with her.

She didn't want to have sex with a variety of people anymore. No, she just wanted him.

She imagined living with him, building a life together. He'd do his share of housework and be considerate of her needs—and that didn't sound like a grand romance, but those things were important.

Nicole had enjoyed herself in the past ten years...until recently. She didn't regret it, but maybe it was time to enter a new phase of her life. Not the crying-and-drinking-wine-alone-in-the-bathtub-on-her-birthday phase, but a phase in which she could let herself be loved well and not freak out when she saw heart-shaped candles.

"Will you tell him how you feel?" Rose asked.

"I'll try." Nicole could approach random men in bars, but approaching someone she knew had feelings for her? It scared the shit out of her. What if he'd changed his mind?

The thought made her ache, but if he turned her down, she'd manage somehow. She could make new friends in her building, and when she was ready, use apps for dating rather than only for hooking up.

"You have to bring him to meet us!" Amy clapped her hands.

"If you're still worried," Sierra said, "about being treated like you were before—"

"I'm not worried about that anymore," Nicole said.

"We'll interrogate him a lot and make vague threats in case he treats you badly."

"Please don't *threaten* him. He's already had to deal with multiple surprise encounters with my family. Don't torture the poor guy."

"You're rather protective of him," Charlotte observed.

Yeah, it was true. He was just so *good*.

Seriously, how had Nicole turned down a guy like that?

Well, no more. She'd throw herself at him…soon. For tonight, she was out with her friends, enjoying this delicious food.

When the waitress brought them another round of drinks, Nicole held hers up,

"I'll tell him tomorrow," she said, clinking her glass against those of her friends.

Rose gave her a hug. "I know you can do it."

Yes, Nicole was ready to make some changes in her life. But these friends, most of whom she'd met back in university, before they were even old enough to buy alcohol, would still be part of it. As would her family, who'd doubtless find new ways to torture her and show their affection.

She smiled before taking a sip of her martini.

Tomorrow.

28

DAVID HAD GONE to bed well over an hour ago, but sleep eluded him. He couldn't help wondering what Nicole was doing tonight. It was a Saturday, so she'd probably gone out, unlike him.

He shouldn't be surprised that she'd rejected him last week. Still, he'd been hopeful, in part buoyed by Murray's encouragement.

Alas.

He should think of something relaxing, maybe recite the geologic timescale in his head, but no matter what he did, his thoughts turned back to her. He wanted her in bed with him. He wanted to make her coffee in the morning and buy her pulled pork sandwiches or Portuguese egg tarts as a surprise. He wanted to kiss her after a long day of work. He wanted to introduce her to his family and see hers again, too.

He wanted, he wanted, he wanted…

But she didn't, and he would respect that.

Maybe, eventually, his heartbreak would heal and they could be friends again. It could never go back to the way things were before, but it would be nice to eat with someone on occasion.

He rolled over and sighed. It would take a while to get over

Nicole, and he wouldn't be interested in set-ups from Murray anytime soon.

More time for reading and swimming, he supposed.

$\sim$

At ten o'clock the next morning, David was back from the pool and making himself a pot of coffee when there was a knock on the door.

He padded to the door and swung it open.

It was Nicole.

"Can you come over?" she asked. "I've got breakfast."

He nodded, even though it was painful to see her now, but he wouldn't deny her.

Except if she was asking him to come over, maybe it meant...

They went next door, and on the counter, where they'd eaten many meals over the last several months, was a cake.

"Mango passionfruit cheesecake," she said. "I hope you're okay with cake for breakfast."

She was smiling as she moved about the kitchen, but he could sense her anxiety. He shouldn't allow himself to hope, but...

Oh, screw that. He couldn't help it, not now.

Especially when she pulled out two heart-shaped candles, exactly like the ones he'd bought the other week. She put them on the cake and lit them.

"David." She gestured for him to sit down, and she sat on the stool beside him. "You know me, and so you know this isn't the sort of thing I'm used to doing. From the beginning, I was very clear about what I wanted, but I didn't expect, well, *you*. I kept telling myself that I didn't have feelings for you, even as you took care of me and brought me a new dessert every Friday. But in the past week, I realized...I was wrong. I do have feelings—very strong feelings—for you."

He inhaled swiftly at her words.

"As you know, I gloried in my single life and feared what a relationship would do to me. I told you that, and you said you'd give me all the space I need, and…I thank you for giving me space for the past several days to figure this out. I feel like you're always on my side, no matter what."

A tear slid down her cheek. He moved to brush it away, but she stilled him.

"After we started sleeping together," she said, "I couldn't help worrying you'd find true love elsewhere and end things, as has happened to me many times in the past. That's why I got drunk that night. And even if I didn't want a relationship, I craved having someone see me that way, just once. Then, somehow, you did."

"Because you're amazing."

"I know, I'm pretty kick-ass." She smiled through her tears. "Still, I felt broken. Like there was something wrong with me— why couldn't anyone feel that way about me? I guess I just needed to wait for the right person to come along. Your feelings are such a beautiful gift. Assuming you still—"

"Yes. Of course."

She grinned at him, and oh, she looked so lovely. "I know we can figure out how to make this work for the both of us. I'm so sorry I broke your heart. Really, terribly sorry—I hate the thought of ever hurting you. But now, I'm ready."

He was, too.

Ready to kiss her.

David leaned forward and cupped her cheeks in his hands. He kissed her deeply. Kissed her for the first time with the knowledge that they'd be together.

It was perfect.

He pulled back to look into her eyes. "Perhaps we should blow out the candles and eat some cake to give us a little energy."

"The candles! I almost forgot." She blew them out quickly.

"Now, rather than cutting proper slices of cake, how about we each take a fork and dig in?"

He agreed, but a few minutes later, he regretted his decision.

He'd prefer to savor the cheesecake, but Nicole was practically inhaling it, and he had to eat quickly to ensure he got his share.

Then she took one particularly slow, sensual bite, holding his gaze as she slid the fork into her mouth and moaned. Moaning almost as much as she would if, well...

"I think we've had enough cake for now." David placed her fork on the counter before standing up. He took her hand and led her to the bedroom, where he pulled her close to him. His attention was momentarily distracted, however, by a flash of color on the wall. "You hung up the painting."

"I did, and I'm thinking of having another one done. You'd like that, wouldn't you?"

"Of course."

"Now get me naked, dammit."

He laughed as he pulled her shirt over her head and dropped it on the floor, along with her bra. He was about to remove the rest of her clothing when her phone rang.

"Ignore that," she murmured.

He was glad to do so.

He swirled his tongue over her nipple, and she groaned.

And then the phone rang again. Except this time, it was his phone.

That was a strange coincidence.

She sighed. "Get it. I'll check who called me and tell them not to disturb me again."

Reluctantly, he answered his phone. "Hello?"

"David! It's Nicole's po po. I just called her, but she did not answer. Can you go next door and check she's okay?"

"I'm with her right now," he said.

"Ah, you made up. Okay, that is excellent news, and now I can tell you both *my* news. Put it on speakerphone."

He did as asked.

"You will not believe what happened!" Po Po's voice boomed through the bedroom.

"What?" Nicole sounded slightly cross about the interruption.

"I was attacked by a Canada goose!" Po Po said gleefully. "Kelsey and I went for a walk, and we were crossing the field at the nearby school, you know?"

"Yes, those geese can be mean."

"Wah, so mean and aggressive. But the babies are cute."

"I think you got a little too close to the goslings, Po Po." It was Kelsey speaking. "That's why they attacked."

"Goslings? What are you talking about? Ryan Gosling wasn't there. Anyway, the mama goose tried to bite me."

"What I don't understand," Nicole said, "is why you're so happy about it."

"Because Kelsey recorded it! I fought the goose off with my purse, it got the message, and it left me alone. People online are saying I am tough. I have so many views."

"I thought you didn't care about that anymore."

"No, I just do not care *as much*. Am no longer trying to be biggest TikTok star. But people say I remind them of their grandmothers and tell me how much they missed their grandparents, so I feel like I'm doing good community service. David, you are very quiet. Are you okay?"

"I am," he said, placing his hand on Nicole's thigh.

"Okay, I will let you get back to having sex. Bye!"

The call ended, and Nicole and David looked at each other in horror.

"Maybe we can wait a few minutes," Nicole said. "That kinda killed the mood, and I actually have a couple of things I want to ask you." She paused. "First of all, how would you feel about going on a real date? Maybe have dinner at a restaurant rather than takeout?"

"I'd like that."

"And the second thing is... You know how you enjoyed hearing me have sex?" She glanced at the wall. "Is that something you want to do more of? A kink of yours?"

"No, I prefer being in the same room as you now—and I don't mean watching you with someone else."

"Good. Because I haven't wanted to sleep with anyone but you in months." She started unbuttoning his shirt. When she tossed it aside, she smiled in appreciation.

God, he was lucky.

An hour later, they returned to eating the cheesecake, and then they went back to bed.

That evening, they went on their first real date. Unlike the last time he'd gone to a restaurant with her—for Valentine's Day and his birthday—he now knew that he was hers.

There was no better feeling in the world.

EPILOGUE

A few months later...

Nicole sipped her drink and took in her surroundings. From the hotel's rooftop patio, she had a beautiful view of the old buildings in Toledo. Dusk was coming, and there were smudges of pink in the sky. The air was hot, and even in her skimpy dress, she felt like she was wearing too much clothing.

She turned her attention to the man across from her.

That was a great view, too.

David sipped his tea and smiled at her, and she smiled back.

It was such a romantic setting, and fortunately, romance no longer scared her. No, she enjoyed getting bouquets of roses and peonies, and watching the sunset with her boyfriend.

And eating lots of cake.

Cake was romantic, wasn't it?

David had done lots of research before their trip to Spain, and every day, he had a new dessert place for them to try.

That was more romantic than anything else.

She definitely enjoyed traveling with him, although yesterday, when they'd been in Madrid, she'd requested a few hours apart.

She'd gone shopping, and he'd visited the Museo Nacional de Ciencias Naturales.

When they'd met up again, she'd been so glad to see him that she'd thrown her arms around him and kissed him in the street, and then they'd strolled through a rose garden and eaten lots of delicious food. Food was something they both liked about traveling.

It had taken her a little while to adapt to being in a relationship, but it was totally worth it, and she had more sex than before.

Including sex on the other side of the Atlantic.

"Shall we order some food?" David asked.

Nicole had eaten a ridiculous quantity at lunch today, and then they'd had ice cream. She wasn't hungry yet; her tinto de verano was enough.

But...

"Yes," she said.

He took his glasses out of his pocket and put them on before picking up the menu.

She'd never tire of looking at him wearing glasses. In fact, she'd never tire of looking at him, period. Hard to believe she'd thought he wasn't her type when she'd first seen him.

Now, he was the very definition of her type.

"What do you think of this?"

He pointed out something on the menu, and she shook her head. He pointed out a few more items, and she shook her head again.

He eyed her. "You're not hungry at all, are you? You just wanted to see my glasses."

She responded with a coquettish shrug of her shoulder and crossed her legs. The skirt slid up a little farther, and she didn't bother to fix it. Let him look.

Sure enough, he did.

But just briefly.

She was certain there were some naughty things going on in his mind, though.

He tucked his glasses back in his pocket, and she pretended to pout.

"Later," she said, "I'll get you wearing those glasses and nothing else."

Just then, her phone buzzed.

"Go ahead," David said.

She took a peek. The text was from Sierra, who was in Paris with Colton Sanders at some luxury hotel. She was having a good time and asked how Nicole's trip was going. Nicole gave her a quick answer, then put her phone on silent. Sierra had been with Colton for almost a year, and last month, Nicole and her friends had finally managed to spend more than five minutes with him. Nicole, frankly, was even more skeptical of Colton now. She couldn't help hoping their relationship didn't last—Sierra deserved better.

A moment later, David's phone buzzed. He looked at it quickly, then set it aside.

"Who was that?" Nicole asked.

"Your grandmother, asking whether I've proposed to you."

"Didn't she text you that yesterday?"

"No, that was the day before. Yesterday was the TikTok of her and Mrs. Dong dancing to a Britney Spears song."

"I don't know how I forgot about that." She paused for a sip of tinto de verano. "Don't give into her pressure, okay?"

"Don't worry, I know you're not quite ready yet." He squeezed her hand.

"One day, I promise." She squeezed back.

"Look at the sky."

She turned her head and nearly gasped. She'd been so focused on her boyfriend that she hadn't noticed the beautiful brush-strokes of pink, orange, and indigo, which tinted the fluffy clouds. David snapped a few pictures, and then they stood by the railing, their arms around each other. The light breeze—a blessing in the heat—blew her hair back from her face.

It had been a lovely day, and she was sure tomorrow would be a good day, too; she looked forward to all the days she'd spend with him, as well as the nights.

"I love you," she murmured.

"I love you, too."

"Want to head back to our room?" She sent him a saucy wink, which, as she'd hoped, made his eyes darken.

"There's nothing I'd like more."

Yes, she was very much enjoying this new phase of her life, with David Cho by her side.

ACKNOWLEDGMENTS

Thank you to my editor, Latoya C. Smith, as well as Kate Pearce for their help with this book. The cover was created by Flirtation Designs.

Thank you also to Toronto Romance Writers, plus my family, for all your support.

ABOUT THE AUTHOR

Jackie Lau decided she wanted to be a writer when she was in grade two, sometime between writing "The Heart That Got Lost" and "The Land of Shapes." She later studied engineering and worked as a geophysicist before turning to writing romance novels. Jackie lives in Toronto with her husband, and despite living in Canada her whole life, she hates winter. When she's not writing, she enjoys gelato, gourmet donuts, cooking, hiking, and reading on the balcony when it's raining.

To learn more and sign up for her newsletter,
visit jackielaubooks.com.

ALSO BY JACKIE LAU

Donut Fall in Love

The Stand-Up Groomsman

Cider Bar Sisters Series

Her Big City Neighbor

His Grumpy Childhood Friend

Her Pretend Christmas Date (novella)

The Professor Next Door

Her Favorite Rebound

Her Unexpected Roommate

Kwan Sisters/Fong Brothers Series

Grumpy Fake Boyfriend

Mr. Hotshot CEO

Pregnant by the Playboy

Bidding for the Bachelor

Holidays with the Wongs Series

A Match Made for Thanksgiving

A Second Chance Road Trip for Christmas

A Fake Girlfriend for Chinese New Year

A Big Surprise for Valentine's Day

Baldwin Village Series

One Bed for Christmas (prequel novella)

The Ultimate Pi Day Party

Ice Cream Lover

Man vs. Durian

Chin-Williams Series

Not Another Family Wedding

He's Not My Boyfriend

CPSIA information can be obtained
at www.ICGtesting.com
Printed in the USA
BVHW061107190422
634699BV00008B/315